LIA PARK
AND THE MISSING JEWEL

LIA PARK
AND THE MISSING JEWEL

JENNA YOON

ALADDIN

NEW YORK   LONDON   TORONTO   SYDNEY   NEW DELHI

ALADDIN
An imprint of Simon & Schuster Children's Publishing Division
1230 Avenue of the Americas, New York, New York 10020
First Aladdin hardcover edition May 2022
Text copyright © 2022 by Jenna Yoon
Jacket illustration copyright © 2022 by Hyuna Lee
All rights reserved, including the right of reproduction in whole or in part
in any form.
ALADDIN and related logo are registered trademarks of Simon & Schuster, Inc.
For information about special discounts for bulk purchases, please contact Simon
& Schuster Special Sales at 1-866-506-1949 or business@simonandschuster.com.
The Simon & Schuster Speakers Bureau can bring authors to your live event.
For more information or to book an event contact the Simon & Schuster Speakers
Bureau at 1-866-248-3049 or visit our website at www.simonspeakers.com.
Jacket designed by Heather Palisi
Interior designed by Ginny Kemmerer
The text of this book was set in ITC Usherwood Std.
Manufactured in the United States of America 0322 FFG
2 4 6 8 10 9 7 5 3 1
CIP data for this book is available from the Library of Congress.
ISBN 9781534487932 (hc)
ISBN 9781534487956 (ebook)

For 할아버지, 엄마, 아빠, Alicia, Bud, Mihee, and Taehee.
Saranghae always and forever.

CHAPTER 1

Left foot forward, left foot back, right foot forward, right foot back. I closed my eyes and moved to the sound of the beating drum. My arms swept through the air as I drew a figure eight using alternating circular motions.

"Loosen your legs, Lia. You need to relax," instructed Master Jinho.

"Ne, Seonsaengnim." *Yes, teacher.* Even before he said it, I knew. Nerves had gotten the best of me, and my legs were too stiff. I tightened the belt around my uniform and took a deep breath to clear my mind.

In front of me, Joon stepped in perfect rhythm with

the drum. To the untrained eye, it probably looked like we were dancing. But this was actually a pretty deadly practice called Taekkyeon, a traditional Korean martial art. Even before Taekkyeon was officially listed as a UNESCO intangible cultural heritage, we've been practicing it for centuries. Keeping it alive.

Joon glanced at the holographic image of Master Jinho shooting out from the silver box in the middle of the room.

Master Jinho clapped his hands and, to no one's surprise, said, "Excellent pumbalbgi, Joon."

I wanted to roll my eyes, but I smiled and nodded in agreement. Pumbalbgi, or Stepping-on-Triangles footwork, was super important, and today Joon had it down.

Maybe I'd be just as relaxed as Joon if my magic power manifested like his had. Everyone knew that if you didn't have any inkling of magic by the age of twelve, it was most likely something that would never happen.

I turned twelve a few months ago.

Normally, I was pretty good at Taekkyeon. But I couldn't concentrate today. Feelings of dread welled up in the pit of my stomach. I knew how all this would end. Not well.

Because, too bad for me, the annual exam to get into the International Magic Agency–sponsored school had three parts: Taekkyeon, academics, and magic.

It really wasn't fair. I was so much better than Joon, but he could do the one thing I couldn't. No matter how hard I tried.

"We'll do one round of sparring," Master Jinho said as he sat down on a chair.

"Ne!" We strapped on chest guards and helmets. I patted my arms and legs. This was supposed to stimulate blood flow and circulation.

After a brief moment, we faced each other and focused on our footwork, swaying back and forth. The key was to maintain eye contact, read the situation, and react quickly.

Joon lifted up his left leg and kicked me. I deflected it with my arm and slapped his foot out of the way. Without missing a beat, I immediately responded with a high kick that landed square on the side of his helmet. Joon fell backward with a yelp.

"There we go, Lia!" Master Jinho leaped to his feet and cheered, giving me two thumbs-up. "Always the fast learner."

Joon grumbled as he sat up. His birthmark peeked out of his uniform, and I motioned for him to cover it. It made him self-conscious, and he hated showing it to anyone. Not even me, his best friend.

He quickly adjusted his uniform. "This is just practice. You didn't have to strike so hard."

"Sorry. I didn't mean to." I reached out to help, but he waved my hand away and jumped up.

Master Jinho chuckled. "That's what the protective gear is for. We must practice hard to be ready."

We stood shoulder to shoulder and bowed to Master Jinho. He bowed back and said, "Keep practicing together. You're both more than ready for the exam."

Red lights flickered on the silver box, and the image of Master Jinho faded away.

After we changed, we sat down on the foam mat and stretched. I reached for my toes and pressed my face against my knees. The backs of my legs burned from the session today.

Joon rubbed his hands together and chanted, "Yakson." *Medicine hands.* Ever since I'd known him, which seemed like forever, he'd always had this ability. Lucky him.

Once his hands started to glow an orangish color, he placed them on his shoulder. The color transferred from his hands and enveloped the injured area.

Even though I'd seen him do this a million times, it never got boring. I mean, how cool was it that he could heal himself? So, basically, as long as he didn't get fatally wounded, he could heal himself just like that. Which was why his complaining that I'd hit him too hard was just ridiculous.

He moved his neck side to side as he rolled his shoulder. "Good as new. I forgive you for pummeling me."

"I should've gone even harder," I joked back.

"Have you gotten your power yet?"

I shook my head and took in a deep breath. "It's too late for me."

"We could keep practicing. Maybe it'll show up soon. There's still time."

Things weren't looking so good for me. People were either born with magic powers or they weren't. Simple as that. It wasn't entirely dependent on genetics, more like luck of the draw. But I had heard that if you were born into a family of magic, the odds of having powers yourself were higher.

I doubted being born to parents with very low doses of magic helped my chances. Appa had an eidetic memory, better known as a photographic memory. A pretty useless skill in a day and age when everything could be looked up on the phone. Umma had the power of—wait for it— flexibility. And she wasn't even that flexible. Yoga-level flexible, not superhero level. So my gene pool wasn't all that great.

All I ever wanted was to be part of IMA, fight monsters, and be one of the four protectors of the world. Of course, normal people couldn't actually see monsters. They concealed themselves well, blending in with humans. Some minded their own business while others, the ones that we were trained to fight—they were the bad ones. End-the-world, steal-your-soul, open-the-gates-to-the-spirit-world type of bad.

I must've been so lost in my thoughts that I hadn't noticed Joon waving his hand in front of my face.

"Why don't you follow your mom to work and see what being a desk agent is like?"

"Won't make a difference. I don't want to work as a no-magic." Technically, my parents weren't no-magics because they did have powers. But, and maybe this was worse, they chose to be desk agents. Why would anyone not use the magic they were given? It made absolutely no sense to me.

The no-magics had the worst jobs ever. Data entry, writing reports, and other boring tasks that required zero powers.

He sighed. "I really don't see what the big deal is. It's better than nothing, isn't it?"

"You just don't get it." How could he? He didn't have to think about life outside of IMA.

I stood up and walked to the calendar hanging on my wall. There were exactly five days left until the exam.

Joon rushed out the door and yelled, "Race you to our hideout!" He disappeared down the stairs.

A large tree stood smack in the middle of our yard. When we first moved here, Appa had been excited to discover it. A couple days later, he bought some wooden planks and got to work building me the most perfect tree house. It was my special place.

I climbed up the ladder fastened to the side of the tree. The inside was a lot larger than it looked from the outside and big enough for us to stand up straight. The good thing about having parents in IMA was that they were able to purchase special magic-infused wooden planks. To anyone else walking past our backyard, this looked like the average tree house. But the inside was a different story.

Joon stood in front of the whiteboard, which was getting pretty full of crossed-out words. We had been coming here for months now, trying to figure out my powers. I had to hand it to Joon for the countless hours of research he'd done in hopes of coaxing my power to show up.

"Today it's"—he pointed to the whiteboard—"intangibility."

I groaned. We'd tried this a couple months back. Definitely not the most fun skill to test out. Intangibility was the official way of saying the ability to walk through walls.

"What is the point in all this anymore?" I rubbed my knuckles. Last time, I believed with all my heart and then smashed my hand into the table. It did not go through.

"Who knows? Maybe your power decided to show up today."

Always the annoying optimist.

"Easy for you to say. You aren't the one getting banged up every time. And . . ."

He finished what I was just about to say. "And even if I did, I could heal myself." Joon chuckled and flexed his arms. "Can't help it. Born with it."

I sighed. No use arguing with him. "Okay. One last time. And then I'm so done."

If this was going to be my last hurrah, I was determined to make it a big one. I steadied my breath, just like we'd learned from our IMA tutor.

The most basic rule was to empty my mind and, if I had a power, try to channel it.

Part of me wanted to prove Joon wrong. But the other part of me desperately hoped that I had some magic. That I belonged. Even a sliver would be fine.

Joon tapped the table. "Ready?"

I nodded, and before he could stop me, I closed my eyes and ran straight into the wall.

For a couple seconds, I must've lost consciousness, because when I opened my eyes, Joon was peering down at me with super-worried eyes.

"Lia!" He let out a huge sigh of relief before starting his rant. "That was such a dangerous move." He stormed to the window and jabbed his finger out toward the grass. "What if you'd had that power?"

"But I didn't."

"Not yet."

"Think it's time you accept it."

"But this is what we've been dreaming about all our lives."

"Dreams change."

He looked at me with a hurt expression. "I guess."

I couldn't stand it. The way he looked like I'd just shattered his dreams.

"Like all agents do, I have a backup plan. So don't worry about me." If I couldn't be part of IMA because I was a no-magic, then I was going to be best friends with Dior. She was the most popular girl at West Hills Middle School, the normal-people school we attended during the week.

Since IMA agents needed to blend in, academics were very important and so most magic kids attended normal-people schools. But because our identities were a secret, we were under strict orders not to use magic or talk about IMA in front of normal people.

Maybe he was in denial, but things were already different between us. After we finished school at West Hills, there were days when Joon would take magic classes with his IMA tutor at his house, while I'd take random skills classes with mine. We used to do everything together.

"I'm going to be Dior's new best friend," I said.

"You know that's the worst plan ever."

"Why?"

"Because you don't belong at West Hills."

Why should I settle for a boring job at IMA while he got to do all the cool magic stuff? No, I was going be the most popular girl at West Hills. And get a fantastic normal-person job someday.

He rolled his eyes. "Okay, so how exactly are you going

to be friends with Dior? Who, by the way, is pure evil. And she doesn't even know you're alive."

I scoffed and opened my desk drawer. Inside was the most coveted bejeweled pink invitation ever for none other than Dior's birthday bash.

Joon picked it up and studied it carefully. A look of disbelief crossed his face. "Is this the invite?"

I beamed but tried to stop because Joon looked so sad. "Always be prepared. That's our motto, right?"

He scrunched his face and shook his head. "I can't believe it. All this time."

I knew he spent every spare moment exploring ways for me to find my power. But we'd exhausted all possibilities, and I was done getting banged up.

"Why can't you just be happy for me?"

He was so mad, his whole face turned red. "Because this is our thing."

"Not anymore. I'm not like you."

"Yeah, but you can still be a part of IMA."

"As a no-magic. No thanks."

"She's just using you."

I flinched. His words stung, but they weren't completely untrue. I got to know Dior because she happened to be in my history class. It started off with me helping her with her homework. But somehow I ended up doing all her homework for her. It was worth it, though, because she invited me to her birthday party. All the girls in her group had a golden bracelet. I had a feeling I'd be getting one too at her party. She was my friend, and soon I'd be able to prove it.

"You're just jealous because you weren't invited."

"Why would I be jealous of a normal-people birthday party?"

What was his problem? I should be the one upset, not him. He was the one who was probably moving away to Korea, while I would be left behind, with no friends at all. Eventually he'd make friends with other people at IMA, maybe even meet another healer. But me? I was the one doomed to live in this boring little town in California, alone forever.

"Forget it. I'm going home."

"Fine."

I opened my backpack and slid the invitation inside, right next to my black leather pouch, which I always carried with me wherever I went. This was my secret stash of nifty things that a good agent might need in an emergency. Since I didn't know any magic, I made my own little collection of everyday items, from paper clips to matches.

CHAPTER 2

For the next couple days, Joon and I ignored each other. During IMA after-school prep sessions, we each practiced on our own. At least today was Friday, and I wouldn't have to bump into Joon for a few more days. I didn't know what to say to him anymore. I thought maybe he'd apologize or show up to my house with another new idea, but there was no sign of him.

I trudged down the stairs. I still hadn't figured out how to ask my parents if I could go to Dior's birthday party tomorrow. It was the day before my IMA exam, but it wasn't like I had a strong chance of getting in. Pretty slim because, last I checked, still no magic power. But maybe they'd see it the way I did. If I was going to stay here with them and continue to go to West Hills, being part of the popular kids group would be a good thing. In fact, it would make my transition to normal-person life so much easier. Dior's party was my ticket in. I had to go.

As I reached the bottom step, I saw Umma's petite frame with her hair swept up. She was wearing my favorite outfit, a formfitting black dress with a big chunky necklace. Whenever we went out, people would always mistake her for my beautiful older sister. Umma loved hearing it. Me—not so much.

I was the exact opposite of her: tall for my age, and I didn't have her dainty features, either. My eyes and nose were too big for my face, but she told me not to worry. Apparently it was in my genes, and I'd grow into my looks. It always annoyed me when she said that. Just because she was gorgeous didn't mean I was going to be too.

Appa reached over Umma and pulled dishes from the cabinets. He was much taller than her and in pretty good shape for an old guy. Appa's black-framed glasses made him look very scholarly and serious, but he loved to joke around and tease me.

I heard my parents talking in hushed voices in the

kitchen. I paused at the stairs and tried to make out what they were saying.

"She's getting stronger every day," Umma said.

"Do you think it'll hold?" Appa placed a bowl of salad in the center of the table.

Umma slumped into her chair and put her head in her hands. "It has to. I can't make it any stronger."

Appa wrapped his arms around her. "As long as she doesn't use magic, we should be fine for now."

Umma leaned her head against his shoulder. "I'm worried. That day still haunts me."

Appa tapped his watch a few times. "Me too. I'll activate the fail-safe just in case."

Umma leaned over and kissed his cheek. "Thank you. All set?"

A beep sounded from Appa's watch, and he showed it to her. "Done."

Daebak. It's a Korean word that literally means *jackpot,* but I used it all the time for when something was fantastically good, or when I was surprised or shocked. I knew I shouldn't eavesdrop, but they looked so serious. Who could they possibly be talking about? Magic and a failsafe? And who was getting stronger? The furrowed brows, hushed voices, and fear in their faces worried me. Maybe something had gone wrong at work, or they had a classified top secret mission.

I sighed. If only.

I didn't know all the ins and outs of the agency yet, but I knew enough to know that nothing exciting ever happened to desk agents like my parents.

Umma lifted her head up and our eyes met. For a second, her face froze before she smiled and waved me over.

Appa turned around and said, "Lia ya, what are you standing there for? Come help."

I walked into the kitchen. My dinner job was putting the food in bowls and bringing them over to the table. I sniffed the air and smiled. It was my favorite today: beef curry with rice. I scooped the rice into three bowls and poured the curry on top. I put everything on a tray and carried it over to the table.

"So how was class today?" Umma asked as she placed a bowl in front of everyone.

"Good. Mr. Baker liked the essay I wrote."

She scooted the kimchi in front of me. "No, silly. Your IMA after-school session."

"Oh, that. That was good too." I stuffed some food in my mouth to avoid talking about it.

"Jalhaesseo?" Appa asked, and winked at me.

The dreaded question: Did I do well? No way my parents didn't know that I still hadn't gotten my powers yet. "The multiple-choice questions and Taekkyeon parts were fine." Actually, I probably got nearly perfect scores on those two sections.

Umma nodded, then said, "Geureom jalhaetne."

"Just those parts went well." I flunked the third, magic portion of the test.

They gave each other a look. Umma changed the subject. "Bap eolreun meogeo."

"I know, Umma. I'm eating." I didn't know why they insisted on speaking Korean to me when they spoke perfect English. They said it was because it was important and it was who I was, but I just spoke English back to them. And eventually we all just spoke English anyway. But every day, without fail, they tried.

My hands felt clammy as I tried to bring up the party. "So I was thinking maybe I could hang out with some friends tomorrow?"

"Weren't you going to practice with Joon tomorrow?" Appa said. "And what friends are you talking about?"

They put their chopsticks down and waited for me to answer.

"My normal-school friends."

Umma raised her eyebrows. "Interesting. I thought you and Joon were team super agents forever."

"Well, I changed my mind. I want to be normal and continue to go to West Hills."

"You're born into this. You can't leave IMA," Appa said as he squeezed Umma's hand. "It's a part of who you are."

"But I don't have any magic."

"That's okay," Umma added quickly. "Just take the exam, and we'll go from there."

I crossed my fingers behind me. "Fine."

Umma breathed a sigh of relief and drank from her glass of water.

"But what about the party?"

"Is Joon going?" asked Umma.

"Of course not. He's not friends with Dior."

"We'd feel better about it if Joon went with you," said Umma.

As if I had a choice in whether he came or not. "Well, he's not. You can't just show up to something you're not invited to."

"I'm sorry, Lia," said Appa. "We can't let you go."

"Please? This is so important to me."

Umma couldn't look me in the eyes. She ate a spoonful of curry and chewed silently.

"Just trust us on this," Appa said in his firm I-mean-business voice.

Tears welled up in my eyes. How could they not understand how important this was to me? "Why not?" I demanded. "I always do what you ask of me. Why can't you let me do this one tiny thing?"

"Because you just can't," Umma replied.

I clenched my fists together and pressed them against my lap. "That's not even a reason."

"Don't talk to your mom like that." Appa never raised his voice except when I argued with Umma.

"Well, she's not being fair," I protested. "I promise I'll take the IMA exam on Sunday. I'll study really hard after the party."

Appa sighed. "Our answer is no."

I wiped a tear from my face. "Just this once, Daddy? Please?"

"No."

"But—"

"And that's final." He put down his spoon and dabbed his mouth with a napkin.

I was so angry, I blurted out, "Well, maybe I'll just go anyway."

Umma shot him a look. "I know you're disappointed, but how about I take you to the Jay One concert instead? I bought tickets for us." She reached out to touch my hand and spoke in a soft voice. "It was going to be a surprise."

Jay One was my favorite K-pop boy band, and they were playing at the Bailey Stadium in a couple months. I had begged Umma for weeks to let me go. She said she'd think about it, which usually meant no. Kind of surprised she actually agreed to take me.

But as much as I loved Jay One, going to a concert with Umma and going to the birthday party of the year were not the same thing. Not even close.

"Who cares about Jay One?" I paused, then added, "I'd rather not go than be caught going with you."

Umma flinched, but I didn't care.

"That's enough, Lia," warned Appa.

"This is so unfair! You guys are ruining my life. I'm going to be a wangtta."

"So dramatic," Umma said. "You won't be a loser."

Appa patted my back. "It's for your own good. Someday you'll understand."

I scowled at them and pushed my bowl aside. "I'm done. May I be excused?"

Umma nodded. I picked up my bowl and put it in the sink. I climbed up the stairs and slammed my door. "Sorry!" I yelled. The door shut a lot louder than I thought it would.

Didn't want to get into more trouble for being rude.

My parents were being so unreasonable.

I pulled out a wrapped box from under my bed and stuffed it into my backpack. I had saved my allowance for weeks and told my parents I wanted a silver necklace with a moon-shaped charm. But really it was a birthday gift for Dior. It'd be really impolite to show up without a gift. Especially since she never stopped talking about birthday presents and what she wanted—jewelry, in particular.

Getting invited to this party was everything.

Being a magic agent sounded fun. But what was the point in being one if I had zero magic powers? And I couldn't tell anyone about it. All being an agent meant was that I took more classes after school and basically had no life. But being a part of this group would change all that. I could be one of Dior's friends and be liked by everyone at school.

As I got ready for bed, a car door slammed shut outside

my window. I raced over to see who was coming by so late.

It was Ajumma and Ajeossi, Joon's parents. In Korean culture it was rude to call friends' parents by their first names, so I referred to them as Ajumma and Ajeossi, which literally meant middle-aged woman and man. But in this case, because I had known them pretty much all my life, the terms were closer to auntie and uncle.

What were they doing here? It was strange that my parents hadn't mentioned a get-together with them tonight. I would've remembered something like that.

Ajumma walked to the front door and hugged Umma before disappearing inside. Appa stood by the door with Ajeossi. They pointed at the sky and spoke in hushed voices.

I didn't know what they were talking about, but I couldn't shake the grave expressions on their faces.

CHAPTER 3

The next morning, I barely spoke to my parents. I refused to acknowledge their dictatorship. Instead, I did the best I could to be just polite enough that I wouldn't get in even bigger trouble.

"Good morning, Lia," Appa said as I walked into the kitchen.

"Morning." I avoided eye contact and spread cream cheese onto my bagel.

Umma hugged me from behind. "We love you so much, Lia, and just want the best for you." She poured her coffee into her tumbler. "You-know-what is in spot number four now."

You-know-what was code for an emergency device that in all twelve years of my life we had never needed to use. Even though nothing ever happened, Umma, in her super-cautious way, still changed the hiding spot every week. There were five locations total. Five! To be honest, I couldn't even remember which number was which hiding spot.

I nodded and kept chewing.

Just then, Tina, my babysitter, strolled inside. "Annyeonghaseyo." She bowed to my parents.

What was she doing here? Tina was an IMA-approved sitter. She had a few tests left before becoming a full-fledged agent.

Umma and Appa hardly ever went on overnight trips. The only exception was when they had to go on business trips. To this day, I still couldn't figure out what was so important that IMA needed to send desk agents out of town.

"We have an emergency IMA meeting to go to. Tina will take you to Joon's house later to practice." Appa hugged me tight.

"Bye." I wiggled out of his arms. A hug wasn't going to magically make things better. I was still so mad at my parents for ruining my life.

✦ ✦ ✦

Tina called me down for lunch. I groaned thinking about her tuna sandwiches. They didn't seem all that complicated to make, but somehow whenever Tina cooked, as in made sandwiches, it just tasted really bad. A simple turkey-and-cheese sandwich would've been fine for me. But she insisted on making me fancy sandwiches. I didn't have the heart to tell her they tasted awful.

To my surprise, there was no sandwich in sight.

"Special lunch for you today." She grinned as she lifted the mesh covering over the bowls on the table.

A small smile broke out on my face. I hurried over to my seat and grabbed my chopsticks.

Umma must've felt bad, because she had prepared some of my favorite foods. In the middle of the table was a platter of neatly lined-up yubuchobap, soybean curd stuffed with a mixture of rice, meat, and veggies. Next to it was a bowl of gungjung tteokbokki. Everyone makes these differently, but I loved Umma's version using thin oval rice cakes with sliced cabbage, mushrooms, beef, and onions, all sautéed in soy sauce and sesame oil.

"Your mom does make the best food."

"She does." The rice cakes were the perfect amount

of chewy—not too hard and not too mushy.

Tina looked at her phone. "Ten minutes, and then we've got to go. I'll be waiting in the car."

I chewed as fast as I could. Should I tell her I didn't want to go? Or pretend that I was sick? But then Tina would have to call my parents and let them know. No, that would be a very bad idea.

No matter how many scenarios I ran in my head, there was only one option: I'd have to sneak away after she dropped me off. One good thing about living in a small neighborhood like Sunnyway was that everything was within walking distance. After living here forever, I knew all the streets by heart. I bet I could walk around with my eyes closed and still get from place to place.

I grabbed my backpack and walked out through the garage. Tina was waiting in the driveway. I hopped into the back seat and buckled myself in.

She pointed to the garage door. "Close, please."

I found the garage-door opener in my bag and clicked it. Instead of giving me a key to the house like normal parents might do, mine gave me a garage-door opener.

Tina pulled up to Joon's house. I scooted out and slammed the door shut. This was going to be the toughest part: lying in a believable way. I was a horrible liar, and Joon could read me like a book.

I waved to Tina and watched her drive off.

Before I could even ring the bell, Joon peeked his head out from behind the curtain in the window. The door opened, and I put on the saddest face ever.

"Didn't think you'd show up," he said in a cool voice.

I clutched my stomach and doubled over in pain.

Joon's voice softened as he helped me up. "What's wrong? Are you okay?"

I kept my head down to avoid looking at his face. My eyes were a dead giveaway. "Ow. My stomach. It must be all the stress."

He opened the door the rest of the way. "Come in and rest."

I scrunched my eyes in pretend pain. "No, no. I just came here to tell you I don't think I'll be able to practice today."

"I'll get my mom to drive you home."

He was about to pull me inside, but I waved his hand away.

"It's okay." I pointed behind his house. "Tina is waiting for me right around the corner."

"Are you sure? I don't see her." He stared at me with a funny look in his eyes.

"Oh, she must be just driving around." *What? That doesn't make any sense. Come on, think, Lia.* I quickly added, "Because it's boring standing still."

I felt terrible lying to Joon. He must've sensed something was off but was probably too busy thinking about the exam to push back about me being sick.

He shrugged. "I guess."

I smiled and waved. "Good luck tomorrow. You're going to do amazing."

"Thanks. You too." He closed the door and locked it.

I waited until I couldn't hear his footsteps anymore. Then I raced down the street and didn't stop until I was a good two houses away. I walked a few more blocks until I reached my favorite street in our town.

Jacaranda trees with purple flowers lined both sides of Arden Street. The drooping branches formed a flowery tunnel. My skin tingled and a happy smile leaped onto my face. This place always had that effect on me. When I was little, I pretended to be a superstar agent searching for hidden treasure in a magical forest.

I stretched out my arms as wide as I could and sprinted down the street, willing myself to go faster and faster. It felt like I was soaring through an enchanted forest while purple snowflakes fell all around me.

Beyond the last jacaranda tree, it was a completely different world. The world of large homes with gigantic front gates. Each house was bigger than the next. The best homes were in this part of town and were surrounded by a billion trees. Dior lived a few homes down from here.

Oh no. In my hurry to get to the party, I'd forgotten to check if I was being followed. That was one of the most basic skills needed to be an agent. Couldn't believe I missed that one. I ducked behind the nearest tree and looked around. Completely empty. That meant Tina and Joon hadn't figured it out yet.

But I was done taking chances. I needed to get to this party no matter what. This neighborhood seriously lacked hidden back roads. But luckily for me, Dior's house wasn't too far from here. All the homes here had cameras, so sneaking around would cause people to get suspicious.

My best and only option was to run.

I took a deep breath and sprinted down the street.

As I neared her house, I hatched a foolproof plan to maximize my time there. I'd give Dior the present, gush over her and the party, and hang out for a little bit. After an hour or so, I'd fake a stomachache and head home before my parents got back. That way I'd still be home in time for dinner and be in a little less trouble. My parents were big on families eating together.

It was a brilliant idea.

Dior's front gate wasn't massive but just tall enough to keep people out. My finger hesitated in front of the doorbell. What if Joon was right? What if Dior was really using me? Or worse: What if this was just a pity invite that I'd eagerly accepted?

My lips tightened as I imagined everyone laughing at me. But at least I could run home and hide under my blankets if it went badly. . . . Maybe I'd beg them to move or send me to a different school. Any school but this one.

Here goes nothing. I took a deep breath and with a shaky finger pressed the doorbell.

The moment of truth.

The gates creaked and opened an inch at a time. I squeezed through the opening and walked down the pebbled path toward the front door.

Just as I reached the front steps, the door flung open. Dior stood there with her hands on her hips. "Lia! You're so late!"

"Sorry. I came as fast as I could." It took every ounce of strength I had to keep from snapping at her. If she only knew what I'd had to do to get here.

I pulled the present from my bag and handed it to her. "Happy birthday."

Dior smiled and took the present from me. "Oh, you shouldn't have." She laughed and threw her arms around me in a bear hug. "Well, come on in! Everyone's in the backyard."

I laughed nervously and hugged her back. "So happy to be here." At least she seemed to be in a good mood.

As I walked through the door, I gave myself a pep talk. *I was meant to be at this party. And I will charm the pants off everyone. And they will all find me irresistible, like moths to a flame.*

Dior's mom sat with her legs crossed in an armchair in the living room. She wore a loose white shirt and tight blue jeans paired perfectly with red heels. No wonder Dior had such good taste in clothes. They were practically clones, with their wavy long brown hair and slim figures.

She waved to us as we passed by and then continued to talk on the phone.

I followed Dior through the house, and I realized that

her hair was dripping wet. Swimming was something I tried to avoid at all costs. I really hoped she didn't expect me to go in the water.

If forced to, I had a great excuse. I'd shrug, put on my saddest face, and say I'd forgotten to bring a swimsuit.

We walked through the living room and stopped in front of the French doors that led to the backyard. I unclenched the fists that were glued to my sides. Whoever said you should try to act natural and smile clearly never had to make new friends, especially super-popular ones. So much easier said than done. I forced myself to breathe in and out—in a very natural way, of course. I learned this breathing technique watching Umma do yoga at home. It usually helped calm my nerves.

A row of pink canvas bags with different names printed in a fancy script sat on a table by the doors. Dior handed me the one that had my name on it. "This is a little present from me. Don't forget to put it on."

My heart leaped. Did she mean *the* present? "Thanks."

Dior stood there and nodded for me to open it.

I couldn't hide my excitement and giggled while I pulled out the contents of the bag. There was a cobalt-blue swimsuit with a scoop neck, a flowery silk robe, a pink towel embroidered with my name, and a jasmine-scented body lotion. Everything looked so beautiful and fancy, although there was no way I was going to get into that swimsuit. I stuck my hand inside and felt the bottom of the bag.

It was empty.

The blue bracelet box wasn't in there. I kept smiling and tried not to look too disappointed.

"Well?"

I was kind of hoping to get the bracelet today. She never promised me one, but Audrey got a bracelet after sitting at Dior's lunch table for two weeks. I'd been eating lunch with her for over a month now. It had to be coming soon.

I gave her a big hug. "I love it, Dior. Thank you so much."

She smiled. "No problem. Go and have fun." Then she turned and walked away to place my gift at a table overflowing with presents of all different sizes.

I pushed open the French doors and gasped.

Outside, a live band played one of the hottest songs, "In a Heartbeat," and I bopped my head to the familiar tune. Two photographers walked around, taking pictures of everyone. A chef cooked in the back corner while kids lined up to order food. There was a long white table with stacks of large and small plates. Next to it were rows of glass cups, some filled with water and others with an unidentifiable pink liquid.

On the other side of the backyard was a white tent. I walked closer to see what was going on. I covered my mouth with my hands and giggled. Girls sat in huge massage chairs as they got pedicures, while another group sat by a table and got manicures. I'd been begging my parents to let me get my nails done for ages. Today was my lucky day.

A group of kids picked out props as they stood in line behind a photo booth near the tent. I cringed a little, looking at the giant pool on the opposite side of the yard with inflatable flamingo and unicorn rafts floating inside. If I weren't so terrified of the water, I'd jump right into those.

A server carrying a tray of mini hamburgers interrupted my thoughts. "Miss, would you like to try some?"

I smiled and took one. "Thank you."

He went off to find another group of kids. At least four other servers walked around with different types of finger food.

My favorite part about this party was hands down the massive dessert table placed unfortunately in front of the pool. In the middle of the table sat a giant macaron tower that Dior had bragged about at school and a three-tier cake decorated with fresh flowers. On one end of the table, there was a platter of pink, white, and lavender cupcakes with sprinkles, and on the other side, little fancy-looking pastries that I didn't know the names of.

It all looked like something out of a magazine. No wonder all the kids had talked about this party.

I placed my hamburger on a plate and piled on some macarons and cupcakes. Umma didn't really let me eat sweets. What she didn't know wouldn't hurt her.

The phone in my bag vibrated. I placed the plate down on a nearby table and pulled my phone out. After making sure no one was watching, I flipped it open. As high-tech as my parents were, they didn't believe in giving me a smartphone until I was in high school. Who knew stores even sold flip phones? They had given it to me two years ago and made me promise to use it only for emergencies and to call family. I laughed out loud. Like I would ever pull out this dinosaur in public.

I hurried inside before anyone spotted my ancient phone. I couldn't believe I'd forgotten to turn it off. Poor planning on my part.

I found a quiet area near the dining room and pressed the talk button. "Hello?"

In a shrill voice, Umma said, "Park Lia!"

When Korean parents say your full name the Korean

way with the last name first, it is never a good thing. I expected them to be upset, but this was a tone I'd never, ever heard before.

I cupped the mouthpiece with my hand and whispered in between coughs, "I'm at Joon's."

"Park Lia, do not lie to me. We already spoke to Joon's parents."

"Okay. Sorry. I'm at the party, but I'll be home soon."

The next words were so loud that I had to move the phone away from my ear.

"Unbelievable. Come home now."

"But . . ."

Before I could finish, Umma said, "I don't want to hear it. You're grounded for six months."

Six months? Was she serious? That was an eternity. *Wait a second.* Surely this didn't include the Jay One concert. "Since we already have the tickets, I can still go see Jay One, right?"

"Of course you can't go."

"That's so unfair. You promised!" The sentencing seemed very harsh for a first-time offender. I always did what they asked of me, except going to this one party. It was just this one tiny time.

Umma hollered, "Unfair?"

I covered the speaker, but she was yelling so loud, I could still hear her clearly.

"You flat-out disobeyed us."

My face turned red, and I protested, "But I was just dropping off Dior's present. You're being so unreasonable."

"Young lady, do not take that tone with me. When we say no to something, it's for a good reason."

I rolled my eyes. What could possibly be the reason for banning me from this party? From having fun? It was ridiculous, and they knew it. They just wouldn't admit it.

"I hate you! You guys are the worst parents ever!"

I pressed the end call button, snapped the phone shut, and shoved it back into my bag. It was rude, but I was already grounded for six months. What more could they possibly tack on? And since I probably wouldn't get to do anything fun for a while, I planned on enjoying every single second of it. Maybe I'd even be the last one to leave.

I made my way to Dior's table and sat down next to her.

Dior stood up and yelled, "Pool time! Everyone, go change!" All the kids grabbed their bags and walked inside the house with Dior. She looked at me and said, "Aren't you coming?"

All the blood drained from my face, and I jammed

the hamburger into my mouth. "Still eating."

She rolled her eyes and said, "Hurry up and go change when you're done, then."

I nodded and chewed a million times before swallowing. There was no way I was going in that pool.

One by one kids in cobalt-blue swimsuits came out of the house and jumped into the water. Dior was the only one wearing a pink swimsuit, her signature color.

Soon a game of Marco Polo began. A few kids closed their eyes and shouted "Marco," while everyone else whispered "Polo" as they splashed around trying to avoid getting caught.

Seemed like everyone was busy. Should I pretend to use the bathroom? Maybe I could hide out in there for a while and come back when everyone was out of the pool. Or sneak away to the tent and get a manicure and pedicure. No one would really miss me.

But of course today, of all days, Dior was in a very welcoming mood. "Hurry up! Come in!"

"Still eating," I said, pointing to my hamburger.

Something about the water scared me senseless.

Ever since I could remember, my body went into a full panic-attack mode when just my toes touched the water. It didn't make much sense. And believe me, I wish it was something I could fix. My parents even took me to see a doctor. It was useless, though. The doctor used big fancy words and said that I have something called aquaphobia—a fear of water.

Thanks, Sherlock, we already knew that. My parents seemed relieved and satisfied with the diagnosis, though. Thankfully, taking a shower was fine as long as I used a handheld showerhead that I could control.

Loud chuckles erupted around me and wet hands grabbed my legs and arms.

"Stop! Stop!" I kicked and screamed.

"One, two, three!" one of the boys shouted. They swung me back and forth and tossed me into the air.

My wails were short-lived as my back crashed onto the water. Imagine a belly flop but on your back. That was me. It felt like I landed on a bed of sharp needles as the pain radiated all across my back. But even that didn't compare to the stabbing pain mounting in my chest.

Each breath I took made it worse. It was instinct to try to breathe. Very bad idea.

I sank deep into the pool with my legs bent backward. My legs refused to straighten and stand up. They were useless. Not only were my legs refusing to cooperate; my arms felt like dead weights that dragged me to the bottom of the pool.

I held my breath, but being panicked didn't help with that. Before I knew it, I opened my mouth to scream for help, but water gushed in, silencing my cries.

My body convulsed as I tried to cough.

I shouted silently, "Umjigyeo." *Move. Legs, please move. Get up and move, Lia.* My body tingled while everything around me grew faint.

My eyes drooped down and closed on their own.

Two strong arms scooped me out of the water.

I gasped for air and spit out water as Dior's dad sat me down gently on top of a towel on the ground. I kept coughing as I tried to get out all the water lodged deep in my throat. My hands and shoulders trembled as tears streamed down my face. Air rushed back into my lungs, and I shivered. There was still something stuck at the back of my throat. Every time I tried to talk, I ended up coughing and shaking.

"Dior, go get your friend some towels," he said. "Boys, to the living room right now!"

The boys followed Dior's dad inside but not without jabbing each other and muffling their chuckles. Before going inside, Dior and the other girls huddled in a corner. Some of their backs were turned toward me, so I couldn't see all their faces. They talked in hushed voices but the backyard was so quiet, I could hear everything.

The girls hugged Dior and rubbed her back.

"She totally ruined my party," Dior said in between tears.

"Did you see that?" asked Audrey as she shivered. "The glass cups . . . they floated up."

"Okay, now who's being the dramatic one?" said the girl standing to the right side of Dior.

"I saw it," Audrey insisted. "They rose up in the air."

"That's impossible," said Dior.

What in the world was Audrey talking about? The glasses looked perfectly fine and were sitting still. If they did rise up in the air, as she claimed, wouldn't they have broken?

"It was probably an earthquake," said another girl, who had a towel wrapped around her. "We do live in the Bay Area."

Audrey rubbed her eyes. "I swear I saw it. Or at least I think I did."

"Audrey, stop it." Dior angrily crossed her arms in front of her. "Can we please focus?"

"Right. Sorry, Dior."

"Ugh. I only invited her because she lets me look at her homework."

I winced hearing those words. So this really was a pity

invite? A bribe so I'd keep showing her my work? I felt like someone had punched me in the stomach and stepped all over my heart. After all that I'd done to get to this party, this was what she really thought of me.

It was so unbelievably unfair. I'd never asked to be thrown in the water. I almost drowned in the pool. And all she cared about was her party?

Nothing had gone as planned today. I was going to charm Dior so that she'd want to be friends with me. She was supposed to give me the bracelet today, a symbol that I belonged to the most popular group at West Hills Middle School.

Today was the absolute worst day ever.

One thing was for sure, though. I definitely didn't want or need friends like this.

Dior strolled toward me, swinging a bag of clothes. "Here, take these clothes. We can throw the wet ones in the dryer."

"It's okay. I should be getting home." I didn't want to be here a second longer.

"No, I insist." She shoved the bag of clothes and a towel into my arms.

There really was no point arguing. She was going to make me change whether I wanted to or not.

"I'll wash these and bring them back to you next week."

"No need. I already wore them."

Dior never repeated an outfit. I always wondered what she did with all her once-worn clothes.

I speed-walked to the bathroom and closed the door behind me. The faster I changed, the sooner I could get out of here. I peeled off my wet clothes and put on a black long-sleeved shirt and jeans. Thank goodness we were the same size or this would've been another embarrassing moment. I squeezed the water out of my hair and used the pink hair tie to put my hair in a ponytail. Then I dumped everything into the bag.

When I opened the door, Dior was waiting for me.

"Thanks for this," I said as I gripped the bag of wet clothes.

She gave me a quick hug, and we walked to the door in silence.

"Happy birthday," I mumbled.

I couldn't have left that house fast enough.

My chest caved in, and I fought back tears. I hated admitting Joon had been right.

I should've known better.

This party had definitely not been worth all the

trouble I'd be getting in. I took the phone out of my bag and gasped at the ten missed calls from Umma. I wondered how many baby steps it would take me to get home.

I had no idea what to say to my parents.

CHAPTER 4

Everyone scrambled to the door to watch me leave. The hushed whispers and cackles of all of Dior's friends dug deep into my already-wounded pride. I shuffled my feet as fast as I could without looking like I wanted to run away.

IMA rule number one was that great agents never let anyone see them sweat. It had become second nature to me. Almost. Okay, I had to try very hard to pull it off right now.

I pushed my shoulders back just far enough that I felt tension in my back. Tears streamed down my face, but I let them fall as I held my head up high. I felt like the models who'd fallen on the runway but had to get up and continue walking. They had to pretend like everything was okay, and I did too.

My cheeks burned, and the tears stung.

No one noticed I was crying because they were all standing behind me. I mustered all my energy and willed myself to keep walking until I reached the street. Dior's place was so big, it took up a full block. I didn't stop to catch my breath until I was in front of the next house and a good distance away from peering eyes.

I'd really thought that even if I had no powers, I could still be somebody by being part of the popular group. My head hurt, and I felt a sense of hopelessness. I just didn't fit in anywhere. Nobody wanted me except for my parents. Maybe not even them. They were probably extremely furious with me right now. Even my best friend, Joon, would be leaving me soon.

All I wanted to do was to snuggle under my covers and throw myself a pity party.

Maybe watch a Korean drama. Oh, wait. If I was grounded, did that mean no television, either? This day truly couldn't get any worse.

My parents could never know that a teeny, tiny part of me wished I had listened. Maybe I was doomed to be a wangtta. If I had some mind alteration magic, I'd erase myself from everyone's memories.

I could really use a clean slate. Too bad I didn't have those powers, though.

In movies, right about now, the main character would kick a can or a rock to take out their frustration, but the streets here were so clean, there wasn't a single piece of trash in sight.

With the back of my hand, I wiped the tears from my face. Whether I was ready or not, it was time to go home and face my parents.

In the distance, the setting sun hid behind the trees, making it look like they were on fire. Something rustled in the trees across the street.

I stopped in my tracks.

Black smoke appeared in the trees and swished through the leaves. But nothing seemed to be on fire, and I didn't smell anything burning, either. Even stranger, the smoke didn't billow up into the sky as you'd expect smoke to do. Instead, it zipped across the street and—poof!—vanished.

A chill traveled up my spine. Rule number two: if something goes against the laws of physics, that's a very, very big red flag.

Time to run. I sprinted home as fast as I could. A million thoughts raced through my mind. But mostly, I couldn't wait to tell my parents what I had seen. They would know what it meant.

I screeched to a full stop in front of my house and gawked at the unfamiliar scene. My parents' car was parked in the middle of the street with both the driver's- and passenger-side doors wide open.

Like they had left in a hurry.

It didn't make sense. They couldn't have gotten home that fast.

Tina's car was parked in the middle of the driveway with the engine still running. Was she waiting for me? She must've figured out that I had snuck away after she left.

"Tina?" But there was no response. I crept a little closer. "Sorry about running away." I paused and called her name again. "Tina?"

I peered into the driver's-side window and saw Tina leaning on the steering wheel. I knocked on the window, but no answer. Sleeping in the car was definitely not like her at all. She was always busy, on the move or doing something.

I stood there, frozen, unsure of what to do next. She wasn't moving at all. I took a deep breath and opened the door.

I shook her and said, "Tina. Wake up!"

The second I touched her, her body flopped lifelessly to the passenger side. I shrieked and jumped back.

Oh my gosh. Was she dead? My hands trembled as I pulled out my phone and saw voice messages from my parents but ignored them for now. I pressed 1 and waited for Umma to answer. Except she didn't. Why wasn't she picking up? I had a sinking feeling in my stomach. I pressed 2 and waited for Appa to answer. His phone was practically attached to him at all times. But his voicemail kicked in right away.

Where were they?

The front door slammed. I jumped and let out a yelp. It was May, and no wind was that strong in California. Rule number two in action again. I covered my mouth with my hands and tiptoed to the door.

I stopped dead in my tracks. What if whoever got to Tina was still inside? But my parents might be there too. I had to find them.

I turned the knob, and the door creaked open. "Umma? Appa?" I whispered.

Oh no.

The minute the words left my mouth, I instantly regretted it. I should've snuck in and stayed silent until I'd found my parents. Now I had just alerted everyone that I was there. Might as well have been holding a flashing sign.

Just broke rule number three: be as quiet as a mouse. I was about to take off my shoes, which was the normal thing to do in Korean homes, but kept them on in case someone was in the house and I needed to run away.

One of Umma's prized possessions, a green vase with two beautiful women dressed in white gowns holding swords, had fallen and broken into tiny pieces all over the wood floors. I squatted down and carefully picked up a shard with a woman's face on it. As soon as I touched it, the woman's face disappeared, and the entire piece turned black. What in the world? I dropped it and stepped back. Umma said it was very special and had been handed down in our family for generations. She hadn't explained why, though.

A sickening feeling filled the pit of my stomach as I made my way to the living room. Chairs were knocked over, and all the board games inside the TV stand had been dumped out. Pillows were thrown on the floor, and even the cushions of the sofa were pulled out. All the books on the shelf next to the window were scattered on the floor.

I stared dumbfounded at our once-cozy living room. This couldn't be happening. Had we been robbed?

Oh my gosh. What if they were still here?

I grabbed a baseball bat from the closet and held it close as I inched forward. It probably wouldn't help that much against robbers, but it was better than nothing.

The house was eerily quiet without the humming of the air purifiers. If someone was still inside, it'd be easy to hear them. I counted to thirty in my head and tried to listen for any noise. All I heard was my own panting. No bad guys—that was good. But where were my parents?

My phone beeped in my bag. The voice messages. I took out my trusty flip phone. Even if they were yelling at me for going to the party, it'd be so good to hear their voices again. I was glad they never listened to me when I complained that no one left voice messages anymore and that they should just text me instead. My fingers shook as I pressed the button to listen.

I heard Umma's soft voice, and my lips trembled.

"Lia. Why aren't you picking up? We're driving home. You need to call now. It's an emergency. Actually, don't do that. Don't come home until we tell you to."

What was she talking about? Why couldn't she just tell me what happened?

There was another message. Maybe it was Umma

saying they were safe somewhere and to come meet them there. I cringed as I remembered the black smoke outside our house. Deep down I knew this wasn't going to be a we-are-okay message.

I bit my lip as I waited for the next message to play. It was Umma again. This time she was whispering and talking really fast.

"Lia. Can't talk long. Find Halmoni and the red coin. An emergency—"

In the background, I heard Appa shouting, "Stop! Stop! I don't know what you're talking about!"

Then the message ended.

Goose bumps rose up all over my arms. As if the first voicemail wasn't bad enough, the second one was downright chilling.

Find the red coin? What was that?

I was pretty sure I would've noticed something like that in the house. We'd lived here for as long as I could remember, and I wasn't beyond snooping around in my parents' stuff. And how was I supposed to find Halmoni? My mom's mom. She lived all the way in Korea. How was I going to even get there? As soon as I found this coin, I'd have to give her a call.

None of this made any sense.

Even though I was petrified, I had to find the strength for my parents. My hands were numb, and they hurt when I pressed them down on the ground to get up. I opened and closed my hands. As the blood rushed back, I felt a million prickles on my palms.

I was a hot mess. But I needed to focus.

Time to concentrate. If my parents had disappeared, maybe the security cameras had caught something.

Inside the living room, I climbed on top of the sofa. My hands wavered as I tried to find my balance. I straightened the Degas painting and pushed three times on the ballerina's face. The wall made a whirring sound and disappeared, revealing a secret room.

This was the Park family headquarters.

I shut the door behind me. No robber was going to get me.

The room had gray walls and five large monitors mounted to them. It kind of reminded me of giant space stations. There were lots of panels, buttons, and keyboards below the screens. Appa was the one in charge of all the equipment in here.

In the middle of the room, there was a round table where we would have family meetings, usually about which IMA class I would take next.

Nearby, there was a pedestal with a tablet mounted on top. I pressed my palm down on it and the monitors flicked on. A red beam shot down from the upper monitor and scanned my face.

I walked to the control panel. On the bottom row, I saw the green button and pressed it. *Bingo.* I'd seen my parents replay the day's footage every night. The screens on the wall switched to the security camera footage. I tapped the back arrow until I saw my parents enter the house, then pushed the play button.

Once my parents came in, they covered their ears as a high-pitched noise filled the house. It sounded like a hundred smoke alarms going off at once. Umma looked at Appa with fear in her eyes. I couldn't hear what they were saying because the noise was so loud, but they pointed in different directions and ran from room to room in the house. Maybe they were searching for something. Then they sprinted out the living room door to the backyard. Trailing behind them was a stream of black smoke, just like the one I saw earlier. The shrill grew louder and then stopped.

A low, raspy voice said, "Bring Gaya the jewel. Then you'll get your parents."

And the screens went blank.

I pounded on the enter button.

Darn it! I slammed my fists on the table. The video clip shook me to the bone. *Who is Gaya? What jewel? Where did that black smoke go?* Nothing made sense.

And even stranger, why would anyone be after us, of all people? My parents were pretty much nobodies in the IMA world.

The mysterious sound itself was chilling, but not knowing whether my parents were okay was terrifying. Whatever it was, it didn't sound human. I tried to think of what to do next, but my mind went blank.

How could I make a plan when Tina was dead and my parents were missing?

I wrapped my arms around my knees and stared at the screen. What was I going to do?

No amount of IMA exam preparations had gotten me ready for this. I'd never seen anything in real life, fought with real weapons, or even had magic. Aside from Taekkyeon, I didn't have any actual training. It wasn't like I could throw a high kick and destroy monsters. I doubted it worked that way.

What was Umma trying to tell me before she got cut off? I took out my phone and listened to her last message again.

An emergency. Those were her last words.

I racked my brain for anything Umma had ever said to do in case of an emergency. All I could remember was "Call your halmoni and go to Joon's house." I smacked my head. How could I have forgotten? The emergency chest. Umma made me keep one in my closet, with strict instructions to use it only in emergencies.

I opened the door and peeked out. Whatever had made that noise didn't seem to be here anymore.

No need to be as quiet as a mouse anymore. I grabbed my backpack, walked out, and closed the door to the secret family lair firmly behind me. I hopped over the sofa and rushed to my room. All the clothes in the dresser were either on the floor or dangling off the drawers. Whoever was here had been very thorough. Even the mattress was ripped apart.

I swung open the closet doors and stepped over my clothes thrown on the floor. I tapped once on each corner of the back wall of my closet with my fist. It faded away, revealing my very own secret room. Every agent had one. My parents obviously knew how to access mine, but I didn't know where their rooms were or how to get inside. I used to complain about how unfair it was and demanded privacy. But here I was hoping that they had been able to get in and leave me a clue.

Nothing seemed out of the ordinary in the room. There were monitors mounted on the gray wall. Below them was a built-in white desk with a standard IMA-issue laptop sitting in its usual spot. On the opposite side of the room, there were empty hooks on the wall. A metal chest, which doubled as secret storage and a bench, sat pushed against the wall.

In case of an emergency, my parents always told me to take all the contents, and get out of the house. I'd opened it once before, several years ago, when Joon and I were trying to find agency objects to put in our backpacks. From what I remembered, there was nothing magical or interesting in there. Other than that one time, I hadn't set foot in this room because the tree house was much bigger and cooler. This was more of a never-in-use computer room.

The bibeon was easy. My parents made sure the password would be something I'd never forget, even in an emergency: my birthday. I pressed 0225. The chest beeped and opened, revealing stacks of hundred-dollar bills, gold, and some Korean currency called won. The brownish-yellow fifty-thousand-won bill had a picture of a woman named Shin Saimdang, who was an artist during the Joseon dynasty. On the green ten-thousand-won bill was an image of King Sejong, who invented the Korean alphabet called Hangul.

I silently thanked Umma and Appa for being so smart to leave behind a secret stash of money. And good job me for finding it. I stuffed as many hundred-dollar bills and Korean won as I could fit into my backpack.

Under the cash were my passport and a smartphone, which I immediately put inside my bag. But there was something else at the bottom of the chest that hadn't been there before: a Korean folktale book Umma used to read to me when I was little. Not for the faint of heart. I was traumatized as a kid because all the stories were so sad. Like the girl who threw herself in the ocean to save her blind father. I cried so much listening to that one.

When I picked up the book, it didn't close properly. There was something stuck inside.

I just knew this was Umma's doing.

Taking a deep breath, I opened the book. My hands shook as I slowly flipped the pages. I took my time because, with magic involved, it could be anything. Or maybe there was a secret message that could only be seen with a special light. My heart fluttered as I reached the last page.

A red coin about the size of a poker chip was taped to the inside back cover of the book.

I picked at the edge of the tape and peeled it off the book in one piece. I was sure my parents wouldn't leave an explosive but decided to err on the side of caution. It looked similar to a transportation coin. Except those were usually silver. On one side were some old hanja—Chinese characters that Koreans used—which I couldn't read. On the other side was a squiggly symbol drawn in gold.

Too bad my parents hadn't left some sort of instructions with the coin.

How was I supposed to figure it out all by myself? I shoved the coin into my pocket.

Now that I had my passport and money to buy a ticket, going to see Halmoni didn't seem so impossible. Hopefully, the emergency smartphone had a rideshare app. That way I could get to the airport. If only I had the power to teleport. Then I could just blink my eyes and be with my halmoni. But no such luck. I had to do this the old-fashioned, very normal, and boring way.

I wasted no time and headed toward the living room.

I froze.

A black shadow lurked in the kitchen. The shadow was faceless and quiet. It moved around and opened the cabinets just like a real person would. I knew I should move, but I couldn't.

This was the first magical anything I had seen in real life. I definitely hadn't seen this in my textbooks, but one thing I knew for sure was that this was dark magic. There was a very distinct foul scent that went along with the shadow. Probably because whatever it was, it was unnatural.

In my head I heard myself screaming, *Move it, Lia! Let's go!* but I was afraid that if I moved, it would see me.

Just running out would be a terrible idea—I needed a better plan than that. After scanning the room, I searched for the best route to the front door. I took off my backpack and slung it across my front. Then I pressed my back up against the wall and inched down the hallway.

Scattered on the floor were shards of broken glass from the vase. Stepping on these would make too much noise.

The only way past the broken glass was to walk around it. Which meant that I needed to peel myself off the wall. There was a chance that this would expose me and the shadow would come after me. But it was my best chance.

Trying to wade through the mess, my hands flailed against a plastic bag. I tripped over it and all the bottles and cans rattled onto the floor. Darn it. The shadow spun around and looked directly at me.

I froze in place and squeezed my eyes shut. Invisibility powers would be great right about now too. I heard noise in the kitchen, so I opened my eyes. It looked around the room and continued to rifle through the kitchen drawers.

Obviously, I was glad it didn't see me, but that was strange. I was standing right there. It should've seen me. Maybe the shadow could hear but not see, which meant I could take the most direct and shortest route to the front door. Just make a quiet run for it, basically. It was worth a shot.

I speed-walked to the open front door. Only eight more steps and I'd be free. My heart pounded as I inched closer. Just as I was about to walk through, the shadow made a loud screeching noise and the door slammed shut and locked on its own. I jerked my hand away and moved back.

Black smoke seeped into the house through the front door and began to take shape.

I wasn't about to wait for the shadows to materialize. I raced to the living room and slid open the door to the backyard. The fresh air had never felt so good. I couldn't believe my paranoid parents had been right. They'd installed a state-of-the-art monitoring and alarm system when we first moved here. Also as backup to the backup plan, they hid an emergency device that was basically a self-destruct button somewhere outside the perimeter of the house.

One family rule that had been ingrained in me ever since I was little was that if anything ever happened to my parents, if our house was robbed or compromised, we must destroy it.

I teased Umma for being so uptight and dramatic. Like anything ever happened here. But I'd like to say I was wrong and thank her for all the extra security measures.

If only I'd paid attention when she told me this morning where she hid the emergency device. I just never thought I'd need it.

I checked under the bushes but came up empty-handed. Then I raced to the lemon tree. Sometimes Appa left little messages or surprises for me under our rock.

Nothing.

Another hiding place was inside the giant blue planter. I sprinted over and dug my hands inside the center of the plant. I pulled out a clear ziplock bag with a note folded inside.

Where was the detonator?

True, I hadn't actually seen it lately, but a piece of

paper? I opened the bag and took out the paper.

My jaw dropped when I read what was written.

Garage-door opener.

No way. I'd been casually carrying around a detonator every single day that could blow up my house? What were my parents thinking, trusting a twelve-year-old with something as dangerous as this?

I scrambled up the ladder to the tree house. Once inside I sat down and opened up my backpack. I very carefully lifted out the garage-door opener. There was only one button on the outside that actually opened the garage. The detonator must have been hidden inside.

I pulled out my trusty pouch and searched for a paper clip. Paper clips were very nifty little tools. In a pinch they could be tied together to lock a suitcase, straightened out to pick a lock, or partially stretched out to use as a screwdriver. I pulled one end of the clip and pounded the tip with a book to flatten it. I examined it with my fingers.

This would work.

Carefully, I stuck the makeshift screwdriver into the back of the garage-door opener and turned it. The screw loosened and I pulled off the backing.

Inside was a small rectangular fingerprint reader.

Whew. There was some security. I felt a little better

knowing I couldn't have accidentally blown up my house.

I placed my index finger on the reader. It beeped and the number ten appeared. Then nine.

I stuffed it into my bag, ran out the door, and slid down the pole at the back of the tree house. As soon as my feet touched the grass, I sprinted out of the backyard, toward the front of the house.

Behind me I heard a deafening blast. The ground shook, and I covered my ears.

Tears gushed down my face as I stared at the flames engulfing our pretty house. I wanted to be brave, but my heart felt hollow and achy at the same time. There were so many memories here. This was where I had lived most of my life. I silently said farewell to my only home. Everything I had ever known or owned was in that house. It was selfish, but I felt a pang thinking about all the Jay One posters I had collected over the years going up in flames. But no matter how I looked at it, this was the right thing to do, because I had to protect my parents. I was sure they'd be proud of me.

But it still didn't feel good.

CHAPTER 5

As if in a trance, I watched the flames engulf our house. My feet felt superglued to the ground.

What I should've asked was what to do after blowing up the house.

There was no turning back now.

I heard the sound of fire engines in the distance. I bet the neighbors called them. This was a pretty tight-knit community. We weren't best friends, but everyone sort of looked out for one another. If a stranger was lurking around the neighborhood, no question someone would report it right away. I don't go anymore, but it was safe enough that kids could go trick-or-treating at night alone.

So it didn't surprise me when I saw people peering out from their windows. The Jeffersons across the street opened their front door and stepped outside. Mrs. Jefferson stood there with a grim look on her face. I couldn't hear her over the fire, but she seemed to be calling my name and motioning for me to come over.

Two fire trucks and a police car, all blaring their sirens, sped up the street and screeched to a stop in front of our house. In my head I knew I should get out of there, but my knees were locked and I couldn't move.

Someone popped up behind me. "Are you okay? What happened?" he yelled into my ear.

I jumped, covered my ears, and spun around. "Joon? What are you doing here?"

He hugged me and studied my face. "I've been calling out to you for the past minute. Everyone's here. We heard a loud boom."

A police officer hopped out of his car. *Please don't come this way.* I lowered my head and turned my back to him, hoping he wouldn't notice me.

No such luck.

His voice grew louder behind me. "Hey! Where are your parents?"

He didn't know yet that this was my house. I managed to squeak out, "At work."

Another police officer yelled, "Connors! There's a dead woman in the car."

"Stay here. I'll be right back." He bolted to Tina's car.

Oh no. How was I going to explain Tina and the house in flames? This was all such a huge mess.

Joon grabbed my arm and said, "We've got to get out of here."

We fled down the street as fast as we could. I didn't know where I was running, just that I needed to get away from there.

There was so much to tell him. Secretly, I was pretty relieved to see him. Knowing I wasn't alone in this never-ending disaster of a day made all the difference.

Before I knew it, we arrived at the playground. I hadn't been here in forever, but when I was little, I loved playing hide-and-seek with Appa here. I wondered if my favorite hiding spot was still there. The rubbery floor of the playground squished under my feet as I walked past the jungle gym. There, beyond the slides, was the little log tunnel, just as I remembered.

"Go left! I'll take this area," the police officer shouted

into his walkie-talkie. It was him again. Why couldn't he just leave me alone? I hurried inside, and Joon followed behind me.

The police officer was now standing in front of the jungle gym.

Darn. In my hurry to hide, I'd left my bag outside the tunnel.

Joon stretched his foot out and swiped it across but missed. The police officer started to walk in our direction. Joon scooted forward and lunged his leg out. This time his shoe caught the straps, and he pulled the bag inside and put his finger to his lips.

I rolled my eyes. Obviously. Why would I make any noise? I stayed quiet as the officer paced back and forth about a foot away from our hiding place.

"Connors. We have an eyewitness," said a voice over the walkie-talkie.

The police officer turned around and said, "All right. Heading over."

Soon the sounds of the walkie-talkie grew fainter. Whew. That was a close call.

Appa's words rang in my head. *Take a deep breath. And another one. One more.* When I was little, he used to sit across from me, hold my hands, and say this to help me calm down. I pictured his smile and soothing voice and inhaled, then exhaled. Even though I wasn't sure how yet, I was going to find my parents. There was still so much I needed to tell them.

"What happened?" Joon hissed. "And where were you today?"

I sobbed into my hands. "My parents are missing and Tina's dead."

"What?" He looked at me in shock as I filled him in on what had happened.

"I'm sorry I lied to you." I paused, then added, "I went to the party today, and it was horrible." I didn't dare tell him exactly what had happened. It was too embarrassing.

I waited for an I-told-you-so, but instead he rubbed my back and said, "Their loss."

I dug around inside my backpack and found the emergency phone. It was a brand-new smartphone.

I tapped on the phone to get it to work, but it wouldn't turn on. The screen didn't have any buttons. I flipped the phone around and ran my finger along the sides of the phone. It wasn't like I hadn't seen my parents and kids at school use the latest smartphones, but those at least had a button on the side to turn them on.

There should have been something on the screen,

but I couldn't find it. "It's too dark here. I don't see anything."

"Take a moment. You've got this." He pointed at a very faint circle near the top of the phone. "Look at this spot right here."

There it was. I raised the phone to my eye and waited a couple seconds. The phone vibrated in my hands and unlocked.

He patted my back and said, "You're welcome."

Before I could make a witty comeback, the phone switched on and a voice message played. It was Appa's voice. "Fail-safe plan activated. Lia, listen very carefully. Find Halmoni's address on this phone and use the map. Trace the symbol on the red coin with your finger. It'll take you there. Be brave. Love you."

I wanted to press play again and hear Appa's voice, but I didn't dare risk the police officer coming back because we were so loud. So this must've been the fail-safe plan he was talking about last night. Never in a million years could I have guessed that they were talking about me.

Joon reached out his hand. "Can I see the coin?"

I waved him away. "I'm all set now. You should go back home. I can't let you miss the exam."

"Are you kidding? That's what you're worried about right now?"

"What about your parents?"

"Lia, stop it. I'm not going to let you do this alone. This is what we've been training for our whole lives."

"Yeah, but the exam is tomorrow."

"There'll be another one next year. Besides, you won't survive without me."

I smiled. It felt great to have my sidekick here with me. My lowest moment didn't feel as bad with Joon around. "I'm going to find the address first."

Several apps filled up the screen, but I tapped on the one that said *Contacts* and searched for Halmoni's address.

Bingo. There it was, written in Korean.

One down, and one to go.

"Now the coin?"

I nodded.

I took the coin out of my pocket and studied the strange red symbol. It looked like a mixture between hieroglyphics and a letter. If it was a drawing, it was very basic. I squinted and tried to picture what it could be. Maybe a head with two pointy ears, two legs, and a tail? It definitely wasn't Korean. I would know; my parents forced me to take online Korean classes every Saturday.

Whatever it was, I didn't know what it meant.

I pointed at the symbol. "Can you read that?"

He cocked his head. "No. It looks like ancient Korean, though."

"Doesn't it look like a transportation coin but in red?"

Joon studied it carefully. "You're right. It does."

I took my finger and traced the symbol just as Appa had instructed.

Nothing.

I handed him the coin. "You're the one with the powers. Why don't you try it?"

He shook his head and gave it back to me. "I think you should follow your dad's instructions to the letter."

I took the coin and dragged my finger over the symbol again. Lighter one time. A little stronger the next.

Joon stuck his hand over the coin to stop me. "Wait. If this is like a transportation coin . . . Remember what our books said we should do if there's more than one person?"

I racked my brain for the answer. I was sure I'd seen this as a practice question on the exam. "Choice C, hold hands."

He laughed. "You would've aced the exam."

"Right." I grabbed his hand and held it tightly. "Holding hands is a must so we don't get lost or separated."

Using my index finger, I traced over the symbol again. And again. Soon my finger moved faster. I wanted to stop, but I seemed to have lost control. The coin started to shimmer. I yanked my hand away and stared with my mouth wide open as it floated above my face. . . .

A burst of light flashed before my eyes, and I felt a warmth surrounding my body. My eyes were wide open, but I couldn't see anything. Had I died? Was this it?

With a thud, I landed on something bumpy and hard. I massaged my legs, which throbbed in pain. Cars honked and screeched. I heard people yelling, "Bikyeo!"

Move out of the way? What? Was I dreaming in Korean? Maybe the flash from the coin had knocked me out.

"Joon?" I called out. But there was no answer. I rubbed my eyes, hoping to clear my vision and find him. But instead I saw the bumper of the car in front of me. I jolted up and screamed.

Somehow I was standing in the middle of the street.

A man swerved around me in his car and wagged his finger at me. He gave me the dirtiest stink-eye and yelled, "Juggo sipeo?"

No, sir. I didn't want to die. Stop yelling at me, please.

And why was everyone speaking Korean?

Joon sat a few feet away from me. I tried to reorient myself. Cars zoomed by but not before honking at us. I made my way to Joon, and then we ran to the sidewalk. I looked around at the unfamiliar buildings with signs written in Korean. Even the license plates of the cars were different. Everyone walking down the street was Korean.

This was definitely not California.

The last thing I remembered was fiddling around with the coin and the bright light. It must've been a secret transportation device.

It was magic! My first real magic.

Well, it wasn't really me doing it, but I was a part of it. I couldn't believe my parents knew some actual magic all this time and kept it from me. I could still feel my legs shaking as I walked away from the street.

So my parents had planned an escape route for me. But where was I?

"That was so cool!" Joon shouted as he pointed at the signs in Korean. "I can't believe we're in Korea."

It was pretty unreal. Maybe I was close to Halmoni's house. I couldn't believe I had really pulled it off and gotten myself to Korea. I'd jump for excitement right now at my first taste of magic if people weren't around. But I wondered how my desk agent parents with pretty much no magic powers knew how to make that coin work. That was definitely strange.

I looked down at my hands and saw that I was clenching the phone in one hand and the coin in the other. Not sure how the coin ended up back in my hand, but I decided to hold on to it. Who knew? Maybe it could help me teleport to somewhere else.

"Is your halmoni's house far from here?"

I held up the phone to my eye to unlock it. A message popped up on the screen saying that roaming charges would apply. I chuckled. A magic phone that still had roaming charges. How cool and strange at the same time. There was so much to learn about the IMA world.

I clicked on contacts and found Halmoni's address. Another screen popped up to ask if I wanted directions. *Yes. Definitely.* I pressed okay, and a map appeared. It looked like I was a ten-minute walk from her house. So that must mean I was in Seoul.

Amazing.

I'd always wanted to visit, but every time I asked, my parents had some sort of excuse. It was almost as if they really didn't want me coming here at all. But that didn't make sense. I mean, she was my grandma. She was family.

It did seem strange to me, though, that even Umma never went to see her mom. And that Halmoni never came to visit us, either. I just assumed everyone was too busy.

A little smile formed on my face and a warmness filled my tummy. Like hot chocolate. I couldn't believe I was finally going to get to see Halmoni in person. Video calls had their limits. Sometimes when I was upset with my parents, all I wanted was a hug from Halmoni to make things better. I really needed that hug today. A giant one.

I held the phone in front of me and walked straight ahead. Joon followed.

The navigation took us past a flower store and a small pharmacy. Then I saw a street sign that read *Pyeongchang 95-gil*. The Korean street names were confusing and really long in English. But at least they were written in both Korean and English.

Not that I couldn't read Korean, but English was obviously easier for me.

I turned the corner onto the street but stopped dead in my tracks. This wasn't technically a street. It looked more like a paved hiking trail up the side of a mountain. I really hoped Halmoni's house wasn't too far up the hill.

Wait a second.

I scrolled down on my phone to look at Halmoni's address again. *No way.* She was house number 250. I looked to my right and saw that the first house was number 1. Just what I dreaded. No wonder the navigation said ten minutes even though I was practically right there. This was going to be a long, long climb up this road.

I didn't know if I'd make it.

Joon walked ahead of me. "Tell me when to stop."

What a show-off.

A car zoomed up behind me, and I jumped out of the way.

The road was steep and winding. This was clearly a residential street. The only supermarket was at the bottom of the hill. The rest were homes or three-story villas. Unlike back home, all the houses looked different.

I jumped across a puddle and past a house with dogs barking. It was impossible to see beyond three houses at this point. I really hoped that after a while, the road would level out a little. I mean, it couldn't go on like this forever, right?

My legs felt like Jell-O. But thankfully, after house 150, the road still curved but flattened out. This I could handle.

Joon stopped and waited for me. I caught up to him and marveled at the massive but beautiful green mountain. I didn't even notice before—because I was too busy focusing on the climb—but the road had changed along the way.

Halmoni lived in a beautiful area; a part of the city surrounded by nature.

We continued to walk. One side now had a railing, while the other side had homes. I peeked over and my eyes widened at how tiny the cars driving by looked from way up here. Incredible view, but more amazing was that I'd trekked up this far. The two things I really disliked were running for fun and hiking.

Okay, make that three. I hated swimming, too.

I'd much rather take a bike or car. It didn't make sense to me that some people voluntarily chose to do this as a hobby because they actually liked it.

The navigation said, "Your destination is on your left," and I grinned.

House number 250. There was a huge stone gateway outside with a blue door. The gateway was so big that it was impossible to see inside. I could only see the second floor of the house and the gray roof tiles.

I brushed some loose hair off my face and tugged down my shirt. It was still my first time meeting my favorite halmoni, and I wanted to look good.

I stood in front of the blue door and exhaled.

CHAPTER 6

"Hal—" I stopped myself before finishing. Just in case the shadows had already figured out this house too, I wanted to be discreet this time. I turned the handle and pulled. It creaked angrily as if it hadn't been oiled in a while. I cracked the door open a little, just enough so we could squeeze through sideways.

A large front yard with patches of yellow, lavender, dark purple, and white flowers greeted me. Halmoni was a flower enthusiast and would go to Yangjae Flower Market every other Saturday to eye shop, as she called it. But Umma said Halmoni always ended up coming home with something, whether it was a vase, flowers, seeds, or potted plants.

In the far corner, a petite but slender figure in a large straw hat crouched down over some plants. From here I couldn't be sure if it was really Halmoni. But my gut told me it was her. I crept behind and whispered, "Halmoni?"

I held my breath as the figure slowly stood up.

"Lia, ya! Is that you?" She turned around to face me.

My eyes lit up as I recognized the smile she did with her eyes. It was contagious. Whenever she laughed, I always ended up giggling. She held out her arms, and I raced into them.

She cupped my face in her hands. "Let me see you."

I looked up into her eyes and knew I was in the right place. Halmoni gave me a big hug, and I breathed in her clothes. She smelled just like I'd expected her to. Maybe even better. For a moment, I forgot about all that had gone wrong and just let myself relax in her arms.

I bet I felt like a big bowl of noodles.

We didn't need to say anything to each other right now. Everything was in the hug.

Halmoni held my hand with both of hers. "I'm so proud you figured it out and found your way here."

"How did you know I'd be coming?"

"When your parents activated the fail-safe last night, I got a message to expect you." Her voice grew quiet and she wiped a tear from her eye. "I just didn't think it would happen so fast."

Of course. Halmoni used to be a part of IMA. Umma said she didn't really use her powers anymore because it took too much out of her. I guess I never thought much of her being an agent, because she was my halmoni. Hard to picture a grandmother sneaking around fighting monsters.

I nestled my head on her shoulder, hoping to feel better, but it didn't help that much. I had too many questions. Where were my parents? How come these shadows were after them? I mean, they were just desk agents, after all. Maybe they knew damaging secret information or were witnesses to a major crime.

Halmoni wiped her face and looked at Joon, standing off to the side near the flowerpots. "And who is this?"

I pulled him over next to me. "This is Joon. He's my friend."

She smiled and hugged him. "That's why you look familiar. I recognize you from Lia's pictures. Do your parents know you're here?"

He shook his head. "I should call them soon."

"I told him to stay," I protested. Ajumma and Ajeossi were going to be so mad at me. I hoped they didn't think I was a bad influence and would forbid Joon from ever hanging out with me again.

"You can use my phone. They must be worried sick." She handed Joon her phone. He walked off to the far end of the yard and pressed some numbers.

Halmoni led me to the front door. "We have much to talk about." Before walking inside, she turned to Joon and said, "Come in when you're done."

I took off my shoes in the foyer and placed them neatly next to her shoes. Inside the house, an elegant living room with large windows showing off a stunning view of the city surrounded by mountains greeted me. So this was Halmoni's house.

"Go sit down over there." She pointed to a large gray sofa and an armchair.

I guess she didn't need that many places to sit. It was just her. Next to the armchair there was a large brown shelf filled with books and picture frames. I picked up the one with the bumpy gold frame and studied the picture of Halmoni, who looked like a younger version of Umma, holding a little girl in her arms at the beach. Umma looked like she was maybe three years old.

Not too surprising that she'd been a cute kid. I mean, she was still gorgeous for a mom.

It was strange imagining Umma as a child. What was she like? I'd have to ask Halmoni this later. But I bet she was a perfectionist and a total rule follower. Definitely not a rebel.

Halmoni turned to leave. "I'll go make some dinner."

"Wait." As much as I loved this little reunion, I really needed answers. I cleared my throat. "So where are my parents? And who is Gaya?" I tried to sound as cool as possible, but my voiced squeaked.

"All the top agents are looking for them as we speak," she said.

Joon walked inside and looked back and forth at me and Halmoni.

I continued with my questions. "And who is Gaya?"

Halmoni sighed. "She's the evil diviner who's been at large for years now."

"I want to help too!" I couldn't believe what I was hearing. There was no way I was going to just stay here and not do anything at all to find my parents. "The voice on the recording said I had to bring her the jewel. Not anyone else."

She held my hand. "It's not what they would want."

Tears welled up in my eyes. "But the message was very

specific. What if . . ." I shuddered at the thought of what might happen.

A powerful person had kidnapped my parents and yet Halmoni was choosing to deliberately ignore the directions. My poor parents. They were doomed.

"But, Halmoni . . . ," I protested.

"Lia, that's enough. Your parents will be fine."

"No they won't! Tina is dead!"

I bet she didn't know that. Whoever this Gaya was, she meant business.

Halmoni's eyes widened and she hugged me tight. "Oh, my baby. I'm sorry you had to see that. But that is precisely why you need to stay here with me."

"But the jewel . . ."

She sighed and organized books on the coffee table. "It's too dangerous. I promised your parents I'd keep you safe if something ever happened to them. No matter what."

What? Why would my parents say that when I was the only one who could save them? But there was no getting past Halmoni on this one.

The shadows that had invaded our home were still out there. "But how do you know no one will find us?"

"As long as . . ." She stopped midsentence and

pinched her lips together. "Trust me. We are well protected here."

What had she been about to say? Her expression gave it away, that it was something important. "As long as what, Halmoni?"

"Oh, I don't remember. I must be getting old." She stood up and said, "I'll go make dinner for us."

I held on to her hand. "What jewel do I need to give Gaya?"

"Don't worry about the jewel. The agents will rescue your parents." Her lips quivered slightly as if she really wanted to believe the agents would find them.

"But why can't you just tell me about this jewel?" Why was she trying to hide so many details from me?

"It's classified. And you don't need to know about it." Halmoni put her hands on my lap. "Oh, honey, I know how worried you must be. But we have the best of the best out there."

So much secrecy. What was so important about this jewel that they took my parents? What made Gaya think I could find it? I definitely didn't have it. If I did, I'd give up in a heartbeat.

I lifted my head and looked at Halmoni. Her eyes were soft and filled with tears that hadn't made their way down her face yet. I could tell she was just as worried about Umma. Why wouldn't she be? After all, it was her daughter.

"You two don't need to worry, okay? Everything is being handled." She hugged me tightly. "I love you so much. Please listen to me on this."

I hugged her back. "I love you too, Halmoni."

After a delicious but awkward dinner, Halmoni walked us over to her study. She had us sit down on the couch.

"What do you think she's doing?" whispered Joon.

His whispering was always so loud.

"Shhhhh."

Halmoni walked behind a wooden desk and tapped on the floor twice. When she heard a clicking sound, she lifted the floorboard up. Then she reached inside and pulled out a long tube.

"What is that?" I asked.

She placed it on the coffee table and opened it. Out slid a large scroll. "I know you have so many questions that I can't answer. But maybe this will help you understand who you are."

I nodded. So this would not be something related to Gaya, the jewel, or my missing parents. Great.

"Lia, grab that block of marble."

I found it on her desk and stood next to her.

"Joon, please hold the end here. And don't move."

He knelt and pressed his fingers down on the edge of the scroll.

Halmoni slowly unfolded it.

It was a painting of warriors fighting against a backdrop of mountains and several hanok, or traditional Korean homes.

"Lia, put the block over here." She pointed to the other end of the painting.

I gently placed it down.

Then Halmoni pointed toward the bottom of the painting. "Do these figures look familiar to you?"

I looked closer at the painting and noticed in the foreground two women in fancy hanbok-type clothes wielding large swords. It couldn't be. The faces of these women looked exactly the same as the ones on the vase we had at home.

"I don't understand," I said.

Halmoni pricked my finger with a needle and squeezed a drop of blood on top of the two figures in the painting.

I jerked my hand away and yelped in pain.

The women in the painting came to life and started moving and fighting. It was like watching a movie. Their movements were so fierce and strong, yet so graceful and beautiful.

Joon scooted closer to me to get a better look. "This is so cool!"

"How did I make them move? Was it me?" It didn't make any sense. I had no powers. And what was so special about these two women?

"You, my dear Lia, are a Hwarang. It's in your blood."

"What? That's not possible." Because according to legend, Hwarangs were the sworn protectors of the kingdom. And now obviously there's no kingdom, but they are protectors of, well, everything. But unfortunately for me, you have to be related to one. And, no-magic me, I most definitely wasn't. Not to mention the other big, glaring reason.

"No way." Joon paused and looked me up and down. "Aren't they all—"

"Men!" I studied Halmoni's face, but there was no sign that she was joking around.

Halmoni sat down across from us. "You two have been studying so hard for your exam. That is true. The Hwarang most people know are men."

"But . . . ?" I had no clue what she was getting at.

"But before there ever were Hwarang, there were Wonhwa, female warriors."

We both nodded and waited for her to continue.

She pointed to the two women in the painting. "Nammo and Joonjeong were the original two warriors."

"Then how come Hwarang are all men now?" Joon asked with a confused look on his face.

Halmoni gently patted the face of the woman on the right. "Joonjeong got jealous of Nammo and killed her. When the king found out, Joonjeong was executed. After that, all Hwarang were men."

I soaked in what she was saying. "So I'm related to one of them?"

She stroked my hair and said, "Yes. You're a direct descendant of Nammo."

I didn't know what to think of everything. How horrible that she was murdered, but at the same time, what in the world? I was actually related to Nammo, a Wonhwa, the original Hwarang.

"This must all be very confusing," said Halmoni. "But there are a few more things."

Joon nudged me and whispered, "Ask her what your powers are!"

That hadn't even crossed my mind. I had a million and one other questions. But since he brought it up, I was dying to know if I had a power, and if I did, where was it? How come it hadn't manifested yet?

"I tried everything. And I really don't have any magic. Does it skip a generation? Can that happen?"

Halmoni smiled sadly. "This is the other part I needed to tell you. Your mother and I are also Hwarang. Not your father."

My mouth dropped open. "Wait. Umma is a Hwarang too?" Well, of course that made sense; if I was a descendant, then she must be too.

"Lia, stop interrupting and let me finish first."

"Okay. Sorry," I said.

"When you were born, your power had already manifested."

I squeezed Joon's hands. I did have a power! I almost shrieked in delight.

"But it was dangerous, because the monsters sensed it too. That you were different."

I held my breath, waiting for her to continue.

"Your mom and I, both our powers manifested when we were older, after we'd been trained in how to stay safe. But you—you were just a baby."

Okay. So where was my power? *Please don't tell me they somehow destroyed it forever.*

She sighed and said slowly, "So your mom searched everywhere until she discovered how to cast a powerful ancient magic-blocker spell on you."

Excuse me. She did what to me? I couldn't believe my parents would take away my power when they knew how much I wanted to be an IMA agent. I'd studied and practiced so hard for the exam. They had no right to take it away from me. If I was as powerful as Halmoni was telling me, then I was sure I could've figured out how to protect myself.

"Magic like that has a cost. To protect you, they left behind everything and everyone they ever knew and moved to California. Your parents made a deal with IMA in exchange for their special protection and new identities: they would go on the most dangerous missions."

Joon grimaced and put his arm over my shoulder. "Sorry, Lia." He turned to Halmoni and said, "Okay. But we've studied everything about IMA. I've never heard of Wonhwa or any female members of Hwarang."

"And what do you mean my parents went on missions? Or that Umma cast a spell on me? With what? By touching her toes?"

"Joon, that's a good point. No one remembers anything about the original ones because they've been erased."

"How can something that important be erased?"

"The memory-alterers deleted the originals from everyone's memory. They've been taken out of books for now. IMA always planned to restore things once the threat had passed."

"But you remember?"

"Only people important to the mission. Their memories were left as is. Your father's mind can't be altered anyway."

I knew exactly what his power was. He never stopped showing it off during trivia night. "Appa just has a photographic memory. Like a big walking computer."

"Yes, but he also has the genes that make him immune to mind control."

Oh my gosh. So that must be why he never fell for my sweet-talking.

"Which made your mom and dad super-valuable and successful agents. They were amazing together."

"So Umma has another power other than flexibility?"

Halmoni laughed. "I can't believe she told you that was her power. I told her to just tell you she was a no-magic. That is most definitely not her power. She's not even that flexible."

Ha. I knew it.

"She's a spellmaker. Just like you."

Spellmaker. Wow. They were the ones who created simple spells for the rest of IMA to use. Of course, the really difficult ones could only be performed by spell-makers.

After hearing this, Joon practically jumped up and down in his seat. "I knew it! You do have a power."

"Not really. My magic is blocked." What was the point in knowing I had this awesome spellmaker power if I couldn't even use it?

"As you've gotten older, the magic blocker has been weakening. Your parents worried about sending you off to attend IMA school. They thought it would be better to keep you safe at home."

"I still would've liked a choice," I said.

Halmoni looked at the clock and said, "Why don't you both go upstairs and get ready for bed? Joon can stay in the guest room, and you can stay in your mom's room. It's the first one to your right."

She shooed us out of her study and walked us to the wooden staircase.

"There are some clothes for you in the dresser." With those final words, she disappeared back into her office.

Once we reached the top of the stairs, there was a random little sitting area with a couple chairs and a black grand piano. Everything looked out of place. Not only did those chairs look really uncomfortable, but I couldn't picture Halmoni sitting there. The top of the piano was covered with picture frames. All pictures of Umma. This piano was probably hers.

Funny. I didn't know she played the piano. Umma didn't mention it when she forced me to take piano classes for a year when I was little.

We walked in silence to Umma's room.

"Good night." I turned the knob and shut the door behind me.

There was a large bed, a dresser, and a wooden desk.

It felt strange to be standing in Umma's room, knowing that she was in danger.

I missed my parents, but I was still so angry with them for hiding magic from me and letting me believe that I had none. It felt like a huge betrayal. Everything I knew had been fake. They could've told me at some point. While I was studying for the IMA exam would've been a great time. Or when I told them I didn't want to be a part of IMA anymore. If they had told me, at least it would've all made sense a little bit. Then my last words to them wouldn't have been so hateful.

CHAPTER 7

For the next three days, Joon and I feasted on Halmoni's cooking, watched enough television that our eyeballs were about to fall out, flipped through all the photo albums in the house, and maybe snooped around a little.

On the fourth morning, just like all the others, Halmoni prepared breakfast for us. Fluffy scrambled eggs, brown rice, several strips of bacon, and miyeokguk, a seaweed soup. She loved to prepare a mixture of Korean and Western foods for us. I guess she felt we might be getting a little homesick, even though I ate Korean food almost every day. Knowing Ajumma and Ajeossi, Joon probably did too. His parents, like mine, always ate everything with a side of kimchi.

I gave her a big hug and sat down to eat. We waited for Halmoni to eat first. At home, my parents said it was okay, but anywhere else, I had to wait for the eldest adult at the table to eat first or else it'd be considered very rude in Korean culture.

Halmoni picked up her metal chopsticks and ate some rice.

Joon ate a spoonful of soup. "Delicious. My mom only makes this for me on my birthday, but I could eat it every day. So good!"

"Any news about my parents?" I asked.

Halmoni smiled. "Glad you like it." She looked at the clock on the wall. "They are still looking for your parents. I need to go back to work. Ne."

Halmoni had retired long ago, but I guess desperate times called for desperate measures. She wasn't on active duty but did what she could operationally.

I watched her disappear off into her study. "She's gone."

Joon got up and slid his chair under the table.

I walked as fast as I could up the stairs and into the room next to Umma's. Joon closed the door behind him.

This must've been a storage room. It was packed full of boxes. Just stacks and stacks of boxes and bins of stuff.

And of course since we didn't have much else to do, we opened and dug through the boxes. Inside we found so much of Umma's past. Things she never talked about, like how she'd been a champion swimmer in IMA high school.

Joon lifted a box off a large stack and set it on the floor.

I pulled open the lid and peered inside. There were books and some pieces of clothing.

I lifted the first book and dusted off the cover, which showed a picture of a golden dragon surrounded by a white tiger, black turtle, blue dragon, and red-vermilion bird. There was no question in my mind of what this was.

"This is her yearbook."

Joon stopped what he was doing and came over to sit next to me. "Wow. That's a real IMA school yearbook."

The IMA logo was unmistakable: the dragon in the center represented kings or gods, and the four animals around it were the four directional guardians. It was a symbol of balance and harmony, and the mission to protect.

I flipped through the pages until I landed on a picture of Umma. She was smiling, with a mouthful of braces. I didn't want to admit it, but her features looked a little awkward, too. Maybe she was right that I'd grow into my looks as I got older.

A couple pages later, I saw a picture of her with a group

of very handsome boys. They all wore jackets with a stripe down the sides. It was a black-and-white photo, so I couldn't tell what colors things were. Underneath the photo was a caption that read *Seoul Hwarang Club wins first place.*

"I wonder what game they played."

"Who knows." Joon sifted through the other things in the box. "Probably something amazing," he said quietly.

I bit my lip. Even if he didn't show it, I knew how disappointed he must be that he'd missed the exam because of me. There was always next year, but still, I hoped he didn't hate me for it. I couldn't bear to lose him as a friend.

He whistled as he unfolded a gray jacket with purple stripes. A blue book fell out from the jacket.

I picked up the book and ran my hand over the dragon emblem on the cover with the "East" hanja.

Joon reached for the book. "Here, I'll hold this while you try it on."

It was the same jacket as in the picture. The one Umma was wearing. I excitedly grabbed it and rubbed it against my face. I smiled because it smelled just like her.

I slipped my arms inside and adjusted the collar. This was by far the coolest piece of clothing I'd ever owned. Well, I guess this wasn't technically mine, but it wasn't like Umma could still fit into it. So she'd have to give it to me.

As I turned to Joon to ask him what he thought, a jolt ran through me. My knees went weak and everything turned dark.

When I opened my eyes, Joon was kneeling next to me. "What happened? Are you okay?" He helped me sit up.

I rubbed the back of my head. "I'm okay, I think."

He breathed a sigh of relief. "I was just about to go get your grandma."

Something felt different. I opened and closed my fingers on both hands. They were sore and a little warm. I rubbed my fingers and felt a spark.

"Oh my gosh. Did you see that?"

Joon nodded and poked my hand. "It's not doing it anymore?"

I rubbed my hands again and flexed my fingers back and forth. "Nothing."

"Well, it could only mean one thing. Sign that you got your power back."

"That's what I was thinking too." No matter how hard I had tried before, nothing happened. This was at least something.

"Let's give your new power a whirl."

Maybe this book would have some answers. I opened it and saw Umma's neat handwriting. I flipped through the pages. Part of it was written in English and the rest in Korean. Pages were filled with diagrams and rough sketches of monsters and weapons.

I showed Joon a page about her first spell, which she apparently mastered at the age of seven. "I think I found my mom's journal."

"Wow. This is amazing and so detailed."

"It's like a manual. Maybe she wanted me to find it." Why else would she leave it here and not burn it or lock it up somewhere? The box her journal was in wasn't even taped shut. Umma would've taken a lot more precautions with the book if she really didn't want me to find it. I had to believe that.

Joon read out the description of the first spell. "The most basic is the ability to move something from one place to another."

I looked closer at the page for the incantation I needed to use. "Idong." *Move.* Sounded easy enough. There were different variations of this spell, like "Umjigyeora," but "Idong" was the simplest.

"I can't believe the ability to move something is considered level one. Doesn't it sound hard?"

"Maybe not compared to the other things you could do," Joon said.

Always seeing the best of any situation. He probably didn't realize he was doing this half the time.

I took off my hair tie and placed it on the floor. "Idong."

Nothing happened.

Was I supposed to be waving my arms and willing it to inch forward?

He gave me a double thumbs-up sign and smiled. "Ready to try it again?"

I stretched out my fingers at the hair tie. In a firm voice, I said, "Idong."

A familiar tingle flowed through my arms, and for a second the hair tie floated ever so slightly in the air before landing a few inches away from where it originally was.

Joon cheered and gave me a high five. "You did it!"

Oh no. I remembered why the tingling felt familiar. At Dior's party, when I was drowning, I tried to will my legs to get up and move. But instead something else did. It must be true what the girls were talking about, that the glass cups moved.

And that could only mean one thing. All this was my fault. I attracted the shadows by accidentally doing magic. It was because of me that my parents had been kidnapped and were being held hostage by Gaya.

But what if I could save Umma and Appa? That would

make everything right again. I flipped through the pages of the journal.

A cockroach flew between the boxes. I screamed and pointed at it.

Joon shooed it away. "Relax, it's gone."

Another thing I hated was insects. Especially this one, because it was a cockroach with wings, which made it so much harder to catch.

I tied my hair and looked back at the book. There was a spell for making something bigger. "Let's try this one next."

Joon studied the page and shook his head. "I don't know, Lia. This is a much harder spell."

Yes. I understood. The first spell was moving an object from one place to another. More like using my gi, or energy, to propel it. But spells like this were harder because I was changing all the atoms of the object. Much more difficult.

But I had to try. I didn't have time to learn and practice the easy spells right now. I needed to master hard ones so I could find one that could help save my parents.

"I can do it. Remember what Halmoni said?" I waved my fingers at him. "That I was super powerful when I was born."

He snorted. "That's not exactly what she said."

I loosened my arms and rolled my shoulders. "I'm ready."

"Are you getting ready for a Taekkyeon match?" he joked.

My face turned red. "Very funny, Joon."

He looked down at the book and read from it. "First pick an object."

I searched the room for one. Maybe a box? Or a book? Then I saw the perfect object. A pencil. I giggled imagining Halmoni's face when she walked into this room only to see a giant pencil. She'd probably be really mad and then impressed by my skills.

"Got it."

"Then say the word 'Keojigeora.'"

"That's it?" I didn't know why I'd thought it would be a more complicated spell than a simple "get bigger." Maybe because in all those movies I'd seen with Western witches brewing potions in a cauldron, they always recited very long spells from a tattered old book.

I stared at the pencil and chanted, "Keojigeora."

The cockroach crawled out from between the boxes and flew over the pencil.

I screamed, "The cockroach!"

Joon peered behind the boxes to look for it. But then he yelled and backed away slowly.

"What is it?" I grabbed the book and inched closer to him.

"Walk slowly to the door."

He sounded so serious.

"Tell me," I said in a panicked voice. Something black and wiry poked out from behind a box.

Joon glared at me and put his finger to his mouth.

Whatever it was kept getting bigger. I opened the door and backed out. Joon followed and shut the door. But before he did, I saw two yellow eyes.

A shiver ran down my spine. "That can't be. Please don't say it was the cockroach." The thing I hated the most and was deathly afraid of.

"You were supposed to change the pencil, Lia!"

"It came out of nowhere," I said. "And this wouldn't have happened if you had smooshed it before."

"How do you even know it's the same cockroach? Maybe there's more and it wouldn't have made a difference anyway."

Ugh. So frustrating arguing with him. Really? How many cockroaches did he think lived in Halmoni's house? She was super clean, just like Umma.

"Okay, okay." He put his hands up in the air.

That was his sign that I had won the argument.

"So, good thing is we know your power works."

"I told you I was gifted," I said in a smug voice.

"I don't know about that. You kind of messed this up."

Before I could answer, something thudded against the door. No little cockroach could've made that sound.

He leaned against the door to keep it shut. "Any chance you know how to turn it off?"

Oh my gosh. Was it still growing? I had no clue how to change it back or make it stop getting bigger.

The creature crashed against the door.

"Hold it down." He ran off down the hall.

I pushed with all my strength to keep the door from opening and ignored the thudding.

What had I done?

Joon brought over a chair and propped it against the door. "Figure something out!"

I flipped through the book, looking for a shrinking spell.

This time, the creature banged so hard that the wood splintered and broke off.

"Get back! Get back!" I shouted. Terrified of what was behind the door, we both scrambled away.

When things couldn't possibly get any worse, Halmoni burst into the hallway. "What is going on?"

There was no use in keeping anything a secret.

The look of pure terror and disbelief on her face was

so much worse than if she had just yelled at me. Then she did something I didn't expect. Halmoni rushed over, cupped my face with her hands, and gazed into my eyes.

"Are you hurt?" She stroked my hair and said, "I should've told you everything." Halmoni rubbed her temples with her fingers and frowned.

Two bony black legs pierced through the door. It was only a matter of minutes before the cockroach was loose.

"This door isn't going to hold much longer!" Joon pushed his body against it.

I looked over at Halmoni, hoping she knew a spell to make the thing go away.

She stepped in front of me and, without turning around, yelled, "You need to go now!"

"I'm not going to leave you."

Halmoni took a few steps away from me and pointed at the grand piano down the hall. "Play C, E, D, and F. Then play C, E, and G at the same time. Hold the C major chord for three counts."

I lowered my head and pretended I couldn't hear her.

"Park Lia! I am not joking. It's only a matter of time before the shadows find us."

"But how . . . ?"

"Once you use magic, they can track you."

My stomach churned and twisted. That must be how they found us in California. Now I'd put us all in danger.

Halmoni walked toward the door.

"Wait! Where are you going?" I reached out to grab her hand.

"When it's over, you run."

"When what's over?"

She moved her right arm up slowly, like there was a string pulling her wrist. Then she dropped her arm and bent her wrist. Just as she brought it down to rest by her side, she lifted her left arm up.

A sickening crack came from the door, and a giant ugly cockroach with abnormally long legs clawed its way out.

We scampered down the hall.

A gust of wind blew across my face even though the windows were closed. When I looked back at Halmoni, there was a mini tornado surrounding her, and blue dust swirled into the air. It ended as quickly as it had started. When the dust disappeared, a little swallow with a blue upper body, an orange face, a white chest, and black wings and tail flitted in front of us.

"She's a shape-shifter," Joon whispered.

I stared in disbelief as Halmoni flew straight toward the creature a million times its size.

The giant cockroach swatted at Halmoni, who soared above it, luring it toward the staircase. As soon as the cockroach scurried after Halmoni, she swooped down to the first floor.

She was buying us time.

We raced to the piano.

"Lia. Come on! What notes did she say to play?" Joon pressed different keys on the piano, but nothing happened.

It was so hard to focus when Halmoni was about to be eaten by the giant creature that I'd mistakenly created.

I stared at the keyboard. There were so many possible Cs to choose from. My finger shook as I pressed the lowest C, E, D, and then F. Then, as instructed, I pressed my thumb, middle finger, and pinky on C, E, and G.

Nothing happened.

Joon shouted and pointed at black smoke seeping in from the closed window. It was the same black smoke that I'd seen back in California.

Oh no.

He inched closer to me. "Running out of time here!"

"I'm working on it!" It wasn't like I was purposely trying to get us killed. I pounded out the same notes on the piano but in different octaves. Still nothing happened. What was I missing?

The smoke gathered into a black puddle on the floor.

There was a blue flash, and Halmoni rushed back through the door. She tossed us our shoes and yelled, "Hold for three counts!"

"Which C?" I shouted back. We quickly stuffed our feet into our shoes.

"Middle." She leaned her hand against the wall and tried to catch her breath. "Creature's in the front yard."

Whew. I got this. I rested my right hand on the keyboard and played C, E, D, and F.

"The shadows are starting to take shape!" Joon backed away from them.

Then I pressed down the keys C, E, and G at the same time. *One, two, three.*

With a whoosh, the top of the piano came off and floated into the air.

I peeked inside and whistled in amazement. A muffled echo vibrated throughout. All the strings and pins that should be inside had disappeared. Instead, all that was left was a dark hole.

The black smoke had now morphed into two shadows. The feet weren't quite formed yet.

"You're doing great. Now go." She waved her arms up and down again.

I beamed back at her, but I froze when spindly arms came at her from behind. The giant flying cockroach was back.

"Look out!" Joon shouted.

Blue sparks flew into the air as Halmoni completed her transformation. The cockroach caught her off guard and struck her. Halmoni fell to the floor.

Just as the cockroach was about to pounce on her, Joon grabbed Halmoni.

I screamed as the cockroach's claws sliced across his arm. Heads were sprouting out from the two shadows. It was only a matter of time before they were fully formed.

Joon cringed as blood dripped down his arm. With his other arm, he cradled Halmoni and ran to the piano. "Come on! We have to go!"

All I could do was stare at the cockroach chittering at the shadows. In a couple strides, the shadows stood in front of it. The cockroach clawed wildly at them, but the shadows grabbed it by the antennae. It screeched as their arms wrapped around it. Soon the shadows were twisted all around its body. The cockroach thrashed its legs, but the shadows tightened their hold.

This was our cue.

I pulled out the piano bench and motioned for Joon to join me. He handed me Halmoni and hoisted himself on top of the piano. I cupped her gently in my hands and rubbed her little body against my cheek. Joon sat on the ledge and motioned for me to pass Halmoni over to him.

The shadows gripped the cockroach, and most of it was gone now. As if they'd swallowed it. Except their bellies would be full. It was more like an absorption.

There was no time to waste.

"Jump!" Joon yanked my arm and we both fell inside the piano.

I tumbled in headfirst. The piano lid slammed shut and hit the bottom of my foot, propelling me down into the darkness.

We screamed as we slid and whirled downward. It was pitch-black inside. I felt like I was in a covered slide, except this one didn't seem to have an end. And who knew what was waiting for us at the bottom? I highly doubted it would be a soft, rubbery playground mat. I squeezed my eyes shut and used my arms to shield my head.

Please, please don't let it be water. Anything but that.

CHAPTER 8

I landed in the dark with a thud on something plasticky and bumpy. The spinning sensation stopped, and I groaned as I tilted my head from side to side. The foul stench of old food brought me to my senses.

Was I in a garbage can?

I gagged and held my breath. The more I inhaled the air in here, the more I wanted to throw up. *Oh my gosh.* Where were Joon and Halmoni? I frantically patted everything around me. All I felt were the same mushy bags that reeked of rotten eggs.

I heard a muffled grunt. It was hard to tell where the sound came from in the dark.

"Joon?" The air in here was stale, and my voice didn't carry far.

Something under me moved, and I yelped. I scooted back and poked the bag with my foot.

"Ugh. Get off me!" Joon pushed a bag off his face.

I must've landed on top of him. "Sorry. Here." I grabbed his arms and helped him sit up.

Wait. Why are his hands empty?

Oh no no no no no.

"Where's Halmoni?" I frantically lifted bags and threw them to one side. I needed to find her.

"I had her just a second ago." Joon put his hands up and pushed up the lid on top of us. A refreshing breeze brushed across my cheeks. The lid creaked and then slammed shut again.

Joon pulled me up. "Come on. Stand up and lift."

I raised my arms above my head and felt the cool metal on my palms. Joon squatted in the same awkward position as me. We gave each other a nod and shoved the lid up as we stood. I felt like an Olympic weight lifter.

The metal lid flipped open and clunked down onto the side of the bin. I breathed in the fresh air. Now I could think and see clearly.

I knelt down and my hands rapidly sifted through the

bags. Joon threw some into a corner. I pulled up the next bag and gasped when I saw the black feathers of a bird's long tail. It was Halmoni.

"She's here! Watch her, okay?" I climbed out of the bin. Then I reached over and took Halmoni from him.

Joon jumped out after me. I scanned the alley, which was full of puddles of unknown smelly substances that were definitely not water.

"Over here!" Joon pointed to a dry spot on the ground.

I gently laid Halmoni down, hoping she'd wake up. But she didn't move.

For once my non-magic IMA training courses came in handy. While Joon practiced his healing power, I'd taken random classes, which happened to also include first aid for animals. Yes. Animals. At the time, I moaned and groaned about it because it seemed like a useless skill, since I didn't even have a pet. Never would've guessed I'd need it to save Halmoni.

I pressed up and down on Halmoni's chest with two fingers. Then I waited. I leaned my head down and checked for any signs of breathing.

Nothing.

It's okay. She'll be okay. This was only the first compression.

I tried to comfort myself. I had to or else I wouldn't be able to make it through to the next compression. And more than ever, Halmoni needed me to pull it together right now. I would not fall apart. I refused.

I pushed on Halmoni's white feathers again. And again.

When I leaned down, I heard a faint breath. Almost like a sigh. Halmoni's eyes slowly opened.

I breathed a huge sigh of relief. Halmoni was going to be okay. I felt like a huge weight had been lifted off my chest. I wanted to cuddle her, but I knew I needed to give her space.

Blue dust floated above Halmoni and soon covered her completely. I held on to Joon's arm as we watched a leg starting to materialize under the dust.

It was working. Halmoni was coming back. I reached over to massage her leg, but Joon held my arm.

I brushed off his arm. "It's my halmoni. I've got to check if she's okay."

He shook his head. "She's still transitioning. You know we need to just let her be."

These magic rules sucked. If I bothered her while she was transitioning, she'd be stuck in a limbo state, not human and not bird. That hardly ever happened with adults, since they had full control of their powers, but Halmoni was so weak right now. It was better to be safe. I stood back and wrung my hands as I waited for what seemed like an eternity.

The last bit of blue dust left Halmoni's face. She opened her eyes and waved us over.

"Halmoni!" I threw my body on top of hers and hugged her tight.

She whimpered in pain as blood soaked through her shirt. A huge gash ran from her shoulder all the way down to her elbow.

I wrapped my arms gently around her neck. "Oh no."

This was all my fault. I'd never wanted Halmoni to get hurt, but now she was lying here drenched in her own blood.

She reached up with her good hand and wiped my tears. "It's not your fault."

This just made me sob more as I held her hand against my cheek. "I'm so sorry."

Her breathing was ragged, but she managed to say, "No. I'm sorry. I couldn't protect you. You were my one mission."

"It's okay, Halmoni. Try not to talk."

"Take me to the pharmacy next door," she whispered.

"Halmoni, you need to go to the doctor." Calling an ambulance was a much better idea, in my opinion.

"It's a magic pharmacy for people like us. The doctor will know what to do."

Joon helped Halmoni up and placed her good arm around his shoulder. I grabbed her waist to support her.

Halmoni clung on and limped as she directed us. "Turn right at the end of the alley."

Once we were out of the alley, the pharmacy was on my right.

"Go in. This is the place." Halmoni leaned on me while Joon opened the door.

A man in a white coat ran over as soon as he saw us. He took Halmoni from us and rushed over to a door behind a curtain.

"What happened to her?" He gently laid her down on a bed and felt her forehead.

Joon explained the situation as I surveyed the room. The medication on the shelves looked like ones that were in a general pharmacy. There was Tylenol, some vitamins, and Band-Aids.

Even though Halmoni said that this was a place for people like us, judging from the medication here, I had my doubts. Shouldn't there be something different for a magic pharmacy? I'd never stepped inside a magic hospital back home, but all the items here I could buy without a prescription at any normal-people drugstore.

"Attacked by a magical creature." The doctor jotted some things down on a notepad.

"It was a monstrously large flying cockroach," I added. He needed to have all the information so he could treat her properly. Shouldn't he be rushing to get her more blood or something? I was no expert, but it looked like she'd lost a lot of it.

He lowered his glasses and said, "But you used magic, correct?"

Joon gave the doctor a look and said, "Yes. Sorry about that, Doctor. She's just worried."

He snipped Halmoni's shirt with scissors, revealing the deep gash on her arm. "You really shouldn't be practicing dangerous magic like this."

He drew a number seven in the air with his finger.

There was a burst of light, and a glass bottle with what looked like tea leaves appeared. It just floated in the air until he grabbed it.

I gaped at the bottle. "Wait. What is that?"

"A medicinal herb." He rolled the bottle between his

hands, back and forth, until the green leaves inside turned into a liquid.

Then he opened it and poured everything over her wound. "This will stop the bleeding and cleanse her blood."

Halmoni's body convulsed for a moment, and then she slowly opened her eyes.

I tried to rush over and hug her, but the doctor stretched out his hand and blocked me from getting any closer.

Behind him, Halmoni said in a voice barely louder than a whisper, "Please. I need to speak with them."

The doctor sighed and checked his watch. "You've got five minutes before the medicine takes effect and puts her into a deep restorative sleep."

Halmoni waited for the door to close behind him and motioned for us to come closer. "When I was leading the cockroach out, I activated the next phase of your parents' fail-safe," she said. "Listen carefully. I'll tell you what you have to do next."

"Can't we just wait here with you?"

"I can't protect you anymore in this condition." She groaned.

"But what about the shadows? Won't they come back here?"

"No, my love. They are looking for you," she explained. "I should've told you earlier, but I didn't realize the magic blocker had broken."

Joon hung his head and shuffled his feet.

"I'm sorry, Halmoni. I just thought if I could learn spells, then I could find one to save my parents."

"Everyone's magic has a unique signature. The second you used magic, the shadows could see you, and Gaya could track you. That's how the shadows found you."

It all made sense now why my parents had hidden so much from me.

"So what do I do now?" I rested my face against her chest and closed my eyes.

"Go to Seoul Station and wait inside Goodway convenience store. You'll see it right as you enter the station. Agent Kim will meet you there."

"Are you sure we can trust this Agent Kim?" Joon asked.

"He's an old family friend and part of your parents' plan. He'll take care of you guys."

"But what about you? Can't you transform and come with us?" The second I said it, I knew how selfish that sounded. Of course she couldn't. She needed to stay here and recover. As long as she was with me, she'd be in danger.

"Don't worry. I'll find you. And one more thing." She flipped her earlobe forward. "Rub behind my ear."

I leaned down and rubbed. Instantly, a hanja symbol for *north* appeared.

"Make sure you check. All agents have one." She looked up at the clock on the wall. "Agent Kim should be there soon. Hurry."

I threw myself on top of her and nestled my head on her chest. "But I don't want to leave you." How could I leave my only family behind, especially when she was injured because of me?

"I'll be okay. I promise." She stroked my hair and wiped the tears from my face. "I need you to be brave and do this for me."

I nodded and pulled myself off her. "I'll try."

She smiled and pointed at my bag. "You have my number. Call me when you're safe."

"Have your phone next to you always, okay?" I kissed her on the cheek.

We waved goodbye and turned around to leave. The door closed behind us with a loud thud. I swiveled around and froze. The curtain and Halmoni's recovery room had disappeared. In their place was a wall of shelves full of generic medication and vitamins.

Joon opened the door, and I followed him out onto the street.

"Do you think you'd want to do that? Be a magic doctor?"

Joon shrugged. "My parents want me to. But I don't know."

I understood what he meant. Umma and Appa wanted me to do so many things, but I didn't agree with them. But maybe they were right. I would've been much safer living as a no-magic. Nobody would've gotten hurt.

"Maybe I'll be a fighter like you," Joon said.

Healers had a few career options. They could train to be doctors or pair up with someone with a different power and hunt monsters. Magic doctors were healers who used the power of herbs, spells, and other magic-infused tools to heal others. A much safer job than fighting.

In front of us, a lady stood at the edge of the sidewalk. She waved her arms up and down until a silver car with the word *taxi* on it stopped for her.

Joon peered out into the street and said, "Shouldn't we take a cab too?"

I thought about it. "No. I think it's harder for the shadows to track us if we're with other people. The more the better, probably."

"Are you sure?"

"It's pretty basic safety knowledge. That's why most agents go off in pairs and prefer crowded public places."

"Right, right. Harder for monsters to get to you. I knew that."

We walked past a bakery, a run-down stationery store, and a grocery store until we reached a bus stop. Joon stopped and looked up at the bus routes.

Students in white short-sleeved shirts and varying lengths of the same plaid skirt and pants stood near the bus stop. A man with glasses played a game on his phone. An older woman in a dark purple dress craned her neck out toward the street, checking the cars passing by. In the distance I spotted a green bus with the numbers 1711 on the front. Even before the bus neared the stop, everyone rushed to the edge of the sidewalk, probably hoping the bus would stop in front of them. When the doors opened, people funneled onto the bus.

"Come on!" Joon pulled me next to him. He held up two fingers to the driver and placed his phone against the reader at the front of the bus.

I followed right behind him. Toward the front of the bus, there were five seats on either side. Beyond that there were four rows of two-person seats on each side. At the very back of the bus, there was one long row of seats. Joon motioned for me to scoot into one of the two-person seats. That was fine. I was happy to sit by the window so I could look outside.

He sat down next to me. His back was rigid, and he had his hands on his knees. From the window I watched the last person board the bus and heard the doors creak shut. As the bus jolted forward, I instinctively ducked my head as we passed the alley that led to Halmoni's house. We leaned back against the seat and breathed a sigh of relief as the bus continued to move.

The bus drove through a tunnel, and everything went dark for a couple of seconds. As the bus exited, tall buildings rose around us, and people walked along the streets.

My first taste of magic (or maybe it was my second) hadn't gone very well today. All this time, Umma and Appa had tried to protect me, and I'd just been angry with them. I'd wanted no part of their world. I resented being born into IMA and destined to life as a boring no-magic desk agent. Sure, you could move up the ladder and become a director, but that didn't mean you could use magic. I'd miss out on all the action.

I'd focused so much on the magic part and not being able to do it. All the fights I'd had with my parents seemed so pointless and petty now. What good was having my power when I'd lost everyone who was important to me?

Everything had happened because of me: my parents getting kidnapped, Tina dying, and Halmoni getting seriously injured.

This was all my fault.

Cars drove around a large ancient gate that stood on an island in the middle of the road. The walls of the gate were made of bricks with an archway in the middle. On the top was a two-story tiled roof with the edges extending up like two big arms reaching for the sky.

Joon stood up and walked to the back exit of the bus. I followed behind him but wobbled as the bus continued to move. I clung for dear life to the bar by the door and steadied myself. Looking around, I noticed that everyone holding on to the little rings hanging from the ceiling stood in a wide stance. I moved my right foot until my feet were about shoulder-width apart. As the bus braked sharply, I felt proud that I didn't topple over.

See? Fast learner.

When we stepped off the bus, we found ourselves in front of a massive glass building with a large sign with blue lettering that read *Seoul Station*. We hurried up the stairs leading to the entrance of the station. Five automated glass doors sat at the top of the stairs, opening and closing.

After we'd entered the station, I saw the white and green lights of the Goodway convenience store not too far ahead. "Let's go get something to eat while we wait for Agent Kim inside."

"Good thinking."

Inside the store, there were rows of chips and cookies that I had never seen before. Back home, the closest Korean market was an hour and a half away, so we rarely went. So buying anything Korean was at the mercy of whatever was stocked in the one Asian aisle at our local grocery store. I grabbed the green shopping basket, filled it with bags of chips I'd never tried before, and tossed in a bag of Honey Butter Chips. My favorite. Then I found the section of prepared foods. It was mostly empty, probably because it was the end of the day. But, lucky for me, they still had samgak kimbap: little triangular packages of rice, mayonnaise, and tuna fish wrapped in seaweed. Umma used to make this for me whenever we would go on picnics or roadtrips. I grabbed two and placed them in my basket.

In the next aisle, I saw a section of packaged pastry buns and added in a few of those as well. Joon brought over two drinks. He put them in the basket and took it from me. He followed me as I searched around the instant noodles section. There it was. I found my favorite, Shin Ramyun, and excitedly placed it in the basket.

"Oof. It's getting so heavy. Are you done yet?" Joon pretended to drop the basket on the floor.

I laughed out loud. "Okay. I think that's everything."

"You sure? You don't need to clean out the whole store?" Joon placed the basket in front of the cash register.

I punched him in the arm and said, "I would, but you wouldn't be able to afford it."

The cashier rang up the items, and I placed them in my bag. Just as I was about to pay, the bell rang and the door opened. A middle-aged man wearing glasses stumbled in. He flailed his arms and walked in a strange fashion, taking two small steps and then three larger ones.

He stuttered as if he wanted to talk, but the words just wouldn't come out of his mouth.

"Li . . . Li . . ." The man stretched out his arm toward me and stuck his other hand in his pocket.

Joon pushed me behind him and ducked back, moving his body away from the man's outstretched arm. The man stumbled and tripped over a stack of baskets. He crashed into the metal magazine rack and knocked over a row of glass sparkling-water bottles on a shelf. The bottles shattered onto the floor, spilling water and scattering glass everywhere.

The man slipped on the water and fell onto his face.

The cashier ran out from behind the counter and squatted down next to the man. "Hey! Are you okay?"

Joon held my wrist tightly, but I wiggled out and rushed over to help the man.

The cashier dialed 119 on his phone and ran toward the door. He yelled, "Stay here. I'm going to go get help!"

"Hey. Hey. Hey!" I shook the man's shoulders, but he was unresponsive. Turning him on his back, I leaned down to check if he was breathing.

"Is he dead?" Joon knelt down next to me.

"No. He's still breathing, I think." Putting two fingers under his chin, I felt his weak pulse.

"Wait . . ." Joon took the man's glasses off and studied his face closely. He rubbed his hands over his own face and let out a huge sigh.

"What? What? Tell me." I shook Joon's arm.

Joon pulled the man's hand out of his pocket. Inside his clenched fist was a phone with a picture of me on the screen. "I think this is Agent Kim."

CHAPTER 9

The thought of prying anything from an unconscious man's hand was pretty scary. I squeezed my eyes shut and tugged the phone. Instead of letting go, the man held on tighter and gasped for air.

I screamed and scrambled away from him as fast as I could.

Joon leaned in closer and asked, "Are you okay?"

The man slowly opened his eyes and turned his head until he spotted me. In a weak voice he croaked, "Lia? Is that you?"

I wanted to talk to him, but Joon held out his arm to stop me. "Identification?"

"Agent Kim. Division One. Magic unit." He tilted his neck to the left. "Check."

I flipped his earlobe forward and rubbed behind the ear. Immediately a symbol appeared. It was the unmistakable hanja for *south*. He was indeed who he said he was. Joon helped the agent sit up. "What happened?"

Agent Kim groaned and clutched his stomach, which was covered with blood. "Gaya. We tried to fight, but . . ."

"Shhh . . . It's okay. Save your energy," I said. He didn't need to finish his sentence. I knew what he meant. If he'd won or found my parents, he wouldn't be lying here bleeding to death.

He looked into my eyes and smiled weakly. "You've grown so much since the last time I saw you. You have your mom's eyes."

This was the first old friend of my parents' I'd ever met. They never really talked about their life before me. I wanted to hear so much more, but right now all I could think about was saving him. "Where's the nearest special hospital?"

He held my hand and said, "It's too late for me."

"But we have to try." I looked over at Joon for support, but all I saw was the grim look on his face.

"Lia, I don't have much time left. I can feel it." His body convulsed and blood dribbled out of his mouth. "Take out your phone."

No time to ask questions. I pulled the phone from my bag.

"You know how your parents are. In case I was compromised, they made another backup plan."

I wanted to chuckle. That was so like my parents.

"The address of the safe house is on your phone."

I scrolled through the contacts. "Where? I don't see it."

"They said to tell you to find the thing you guys love doing together every year."

I knew exactly what he was talking about. Every birthday, for as long as I could remember, instead of giving me presents the normal way, my parents would plan out an entire treasure hunt. I swiped through the phone and found an app with a birthday cake icon. I'd seen this earlier but thought it was to keep track of birthdays. As soon as I tapped, it asked for a password.

I smiled. The bibeon could only be one thing. Before opening my treasure, we had a ritual. I had to yell "boom, boom, boom" and do a short dance before I got to see what I had found. As I got older, I begged them not to make me do it anymore, but they just laughed and said it was our little tradition.

I typed *boom boom boom* and pressed enter.

An address appeared on the screen.

"I got it!" I flashed the phone to Agent Kim.

He pulled the phone closer. "This is in Busan. Get on the next train."

Even though I was terrified that we were now on our own, I wanted to reassure Agent Kim. In a brave voice I said, "We will. Don't worry about us."

"Your parents always said you were special," Agent Kim said in between coughs. "When you meet them, tell them I'm sorry I failed them."

I rested my head against his chest and hugged him. "You tried your best. And you found me. That's what I'll tell them."

He took a deep breath and whispered, "And remember: whatever you see next, whatever happens next, it's not me."

"What do you mean?" When I looked up at his face, his eyes were closed. I shook his shoulders. "Agent Kim? Agent Kim?"

Joon stood and tried to pull me up. "Come on, we have to go."

I held his hand but felt a chill run through my body.

I slowly looked down and screamed.

A watery hand wrapped its long fingers around my ankle. The hand came out from the puddle on the floor next to Agent Kim's body.

Joon yanked on my arm, but the pressure on my leg was too strong. I felt the fingers squeezing my ankle, almost cutting off my circulation.

"Get it off me!" I twisted and squirmed.

"Hold on!" Joon yelled. He tried to pry the fingers off. "I can't. It's too strong!"

My leg grew numb, and I couldn't move. "Help me!"

Joon knelt down and grunted as he tried to lift the index finger up.

But it didn't budge.

Instead it tightened its grip, and I yelped in pain. I leaned forward and clung to Joon, hoping he could drag me away, but I slipped and fell onto my back while my other leg landed in the puddle.

I propped myself back up, but another hand slithered out from the puddle and latched onto my wrist. My eyes bulged and I shrieked.

In full panic mode, with my other foot I kicked the hand on my ankle and thrashed my arm, but it was all useless.

Tears streamed down my face.

"Use your power."

"Gaya will find me," I blubbered back.

"She already has. Use it or we'll both be captured."

"I only know two spells," I said in a raspy breath.

"Figure it out!" he shouted, too close to my ear.

I squeezed my eyes shut and saw flashbacks of Halmoni and the giant cockroach that injured her. I clearly didn't know what I was doing.

But I had to try. I didn't want this to be the end.

I took a deep breath and pictured the fingers bending backward. *A little more.* I chanted "Idong." But nothing happened. I tried the other spell for *move* and said, "Umjigyeora" as I willed the fingers to lift little by little. I focused on the thumb and imagined it unbending and straightening.

Joon squealed in pain as he clutched his hand. "Not mine!"

"Sorry!" I closed my eyes and tried again. This time I focused on the bony fingers around my ankle and willed them to lift as I chanted, "Umjigyeora."

Joon squeezed my shoulder and I gasped when the thumb lifted slightly off my ankle. It was just enough space for me to wiggle my foot out. The grip around my wrist loosened too, as if the hand was startled by what had just happened.

This was all I needed. Joon grabbed my wrist and toppled over backward. We scooted as fast as we could and hid behind an aisle of food.

The hands clenched into fists and banged on the floor. Then they slowly opened and closed in front of Agent Kim's face. Black smoke seeped out from his ears. The palms of the hands faced the ceiling and the fingers curled in and then out again.

Huddled behind the aisle, we watched in horror as the two streams of smoke weaved around each other like a twisted Korean doughnut, convulsing and spiraling.

"Run!" I pushed Joon toward the door. There was no point watching anymore because I knew what the smoke would become. A shadow. I just hadn't known it would come out of Agent Kim's body.

As we sprinted out, a group of paramedics and police burst into the store.

"Wait! Don't go in!" I whirled around and started to chase after them. "We have to warn them!"

Joon grabbed my arm and pulled me back. "Let them go. The shadows aren't after them."

Very true. So far, the shadows had been mission-minded and specific in terms of their target. Namely me.

We raced past the ticket booth and skidded right toward the train tracks.

"Don't we need tickets?" I yelled.

"No time!" he yelled back.

I panted, chasing after him. "Do you even know where we're going?"

He pointed up at the signs for the train tracks. "The address said Busan. That's number fourteen."

I thought I felt something lurking behind me. The air turned cold around me just for a couple seconds, and I rubbed my hands together. Joon must have sensed it too because he said, "Run faster!"

A group of commuters speed-walked past us, and without missing a beat, we ran after them. I figured as long as we were with a big group of people, it'd be harder for the shadows to find me.

The group began to dwindle as three people split off and went down the stairs to track eleven.

Joon nudged me and said, "Let's make a run for it."

I breathed a sigh of relief that the shadows hadn't found us yet. Running sounded like a good plan. We needed to get out of here fast.

We sprinted and weaved past the people. *Track twelve. Track thirteen.*

At track fourteen, we raced down the stairs.

I looked behind me and thought I saw something dark lurking near the walls. The station wasn't well lit, so it was hard to tell whether the shadows had followed us.

A drop of water landed on my head. And another on my jacket. I looked up to see if there was anything there. Nothing.

Something tugged on my jacket and I turned around, but no one was there. I patted my jacket and pockets, but there was nothing there. A chill went up my spine, and I sensed something wasn't right, but I couldn't put my finger on it.

"Hurry up, Lia!" Joon yelled from the bottom of the stairs.

I shivered and ran down the last few steps.

Attendants stood at different areas on the platform, helping people with their tickets. I panicked. "What now?"

Joon tilted his head and said, "Follow me."

The car in front of us had a number three, and the one to the right of it had a number two on it. Joon turned to walk the other way. There was a long line at the newspaper stand in front of car number four. Walking around the line, we continued to car number five, which didn't have an attendant standing out front. Once we climbed aboard, we entered the cabin.

Joon walked down the aisle all the way to the other

end of the car and slid into a seat. I sat down next to him.

The doors closed, and the train started to move.

"Don't they check tickets here?" I felt uneasy as the people seated around us took out their tickets. "Maybe we can say we lost ours?"

"Relax. The attendant will come around soon enough."

"What? How is that a good thing?"

"Because we can buy tickets from the attendant." He paused, and then said, "You do have money, right?"

Good thing I'd had the sense to pack all the cash my parents stashed away. "A whole bagful."

"Great. Because I only have the regular public transportation pass on my phone. It doesn't have nearly enough on there to cover this trip."

"Are you sure we won't get kicked off?" I asked.

"Pretty sure. The last time I rode the train with my parents, I saw someone buy a ticket on the spot."

Pretty sure that was not the same as 100 percent definitely sure. I leaned back in my chair and clutched my bag.

A lady dressed in a little hat, gray blazer, and skirt entered through the doors of the cabin. She walked from aisle to aisle, smiling and checking tickets.

My heart beat faster. What if this didn't work?

She stood in front of Joon. "Tickets, please."

He smiled and said, "I'm so sorry. We rushed on and forgot to buy our tickets."

She frowned and looked down at her tablet. "Okay. Where are you headed?"

"To Busan." I leaned over and gazed at her with the saddest eyes I could manage. "We really need to get there. Can we pay now, please?"

She tapped on her tablet and said, "Lucky for you, it's not completely sold out."

I smiled and clasped my hands together in front of me. "Thank you."

"I can make an exception for you this time. But next time you have to buy your tickets at the counter."

"We will. Thank you." Joon nudged me and pointed to my bag.

I unzipped my bag. "How much is it?"

"For the two of you, it's one hundred twenty thousand won."

I pulled out two fifty-thousand-won bills and two ten-thousand-won bills from my bag and handed them to her.

She took the money and gave me two tickets. "Enjoy your trip."

As soon as she left, Joon said, "See? I told you it would work."

So glad he was right about this one. My eyes drooped, and I covered my mouth to yawn. It must be really late at night back home. I pulled down the tray table, folded my arms on top of it, and rested my head.

Joon took off his jacket and placed it on me like a blanket. "I'll wake you up when we get there. It's about a three-hour ride."

I nodded and closed my eyes.

CHAPTER 10

As much as I wanted to, it was hard to fall asleep with so many things running through my mind. Right now our biggest problems were that we were alone and left to fend for ourselves, and had to somehow find and rescue my parents. Not to mention defeat Gaya in the process. I couldn't shake the feeling that I'd seen those hands somewhere before. The sensation of sinking and being pulled by those hands struck a chord in me that I didn't know I had.

I peeked my head up and found Joon leaning his head back with his eyes closed.

"Joon, are you sleeping?" I asked.

"No. Just resting my eyes," he mumbled.

I reached over and shook his shoulder. "Can you wake up, please?"

He groaned and opened his eyes. "Okay. I'm up."

"So do you think Agent Kim . . ." I looked around and continued in a low voice, "Is a shadow now?"

He nodded. "I don't know how Gaya does it. But I think the shadows were actually people."

That did make sense. We'd seen smoke coming out of his body. And we knew now that the smoke eventually morphed into a shadow. It was wishful thinking, but I needed to know if there was even a slight chance he could still be saved somehow.

"But do you think he's really dead? Maybe there's a way to bring him back."

"He's totally dead. That shadow didn't recognize us at all. Remember the last thing he said to us?" Joon closed his eyes. "Get some rest."

Agent Kim's last words repeated in my head. That was what he must've meant. That the shadow was not him. I looked out the window at the open fields and mountains with a couple little houses scattered in between.

Joon didn't seem too concerned about what had just happened. Or he was just really good at hiding his feelings. It wasn't like I'd known Agent Kim very well, but he had known my parents. I said a silent goodbye to him. Guess it was just the two of us now.

I must've dozed off, because a loud beeping sound made me jump in my seat. I rubbed my eyes and listened to a woman on the speaker. "The next stop is Busan station. This is the last stop." The man in front of me stood up and reached for his bag in the overhead compartment. Other people scooted into the aisle and walked toward the door.

Joon clasped his hands together, stretched his arms up, and wiggled his body to the left and the right. He looked over at me and said, "You ready?"

I nodded and nudged him to start moving. We followed the crowd of people and got off the train. It was a pretty small train station, and everyone flocked to the one staircase. At the top of the staircase there was a coffee shop, a convenience store, and several doors leading outside.

As I breathed in the air, a sharp pain pierced through my head. I closed my eyes to quiet the pain but couldn't focus because of a crying child. The cries sounded familiar, like I'd heard them somewhere before. I looked around the station, but there was no one around me except for Joon. It was strange, but maybe I was just overtired. It had been a long day.

I fiddled with my phone and entered the safe house address into the navigation.

"Do you know how to get there?" he asked.

I flashed Joon the directions.

"Come on. This way." I waved my hand in the air and pointed to exit number three.

Outside there was a line of people waiting to catch a taxi. A little farther down, people climbed onto buses. By now I knew better than to think we would take a comfortable cab ride to the safe house.

I really hoped the walk to this place was short.

We passed a couple of closed stores and turned into a small alley. The streetlamp flickered and made the house numbers hard to see, but Joon kept walking. I looked up and breathed a sigh of relief that this road wasn't uphill like the one to Halmoni's house. Thank goodness for that. My body definitely couldn't handle another hike right now.

My phone beeped, signaling that we were near the destination. All I saw was a run-down house that looked really unsafe to walk into. The roof was coming apart, some windows were broken, and the paint was peeling off. I'm not sure what I imagined a safe house would look like, but it should at least be functional and look livable.

There was no need to even bother with the joke of a lock, because the door wouldn't shut properly.

The door creaked open, and I sneezed. There was so much dust in this place. I bet no one had been here in a long time. Joon seemed unfazed and walked inside confidently.

"This place is amazing. No one would suspect it at all."

He was right. No one would think twice about this place.

The navigation should've turned off, but it continued to direct us. "Uh. This way," I said nervously. We walked down the hallway and turned a corner that led us into the kitchen.

"How are there still more directions when we've already arrived?" asked Joon.

"Magic?" I answered half-jokingly. It didn't make sense, but maybe there were two addresses for this place?

I took a few steps forward and stood in front of a pantry door.

Joon peered over at my phone. "Looks like it wants us to go in."

Once we stepped inside the pantry, there were shelves on two of the walls, but on what should've been a third wall was a door.

Oddly enough, this door looked eerily similar to the one in my closet. It didn't match the rest of the house and had clearly been updated. It was worth a shot. I tapped once on each corner of the door. There was a soft whoosh. The door disappeared and in its place was a metal gate with a scanner embedded into it.

"What now?" Joon asked.

Amazing. Just like the one in our family headquarters. We were definitely in the right place.

"Now this." I trusted my instinct and placed my palm on the scanner.

Even though I was sure this would work, I still worried. What if I was wrong and I accidentally triggered Umma's intruder mode? I shuddered at the thought. This was my family's place; they would've entered my prints as well on the sensor. Right? Unless they were too busy or lazy and forgot over all these years. My hand kept trembling, so Joon laid his hand on top of mine to steady it. I froze, then hid my head behind his shoulder.

There was a bright flash of light and a loud creaking sound as the metal gate lifted up. I peeked under the door. The lights dangling from the ceiling came on, revealing a wooden staircase.

Joon took the lead and went down the stairs. It wasn't

that I was too chicken to follow after him, but I was just taking a moment to admire my parents' handiwork.

"Come down! It's safe."

I raced down the stairs and was greeted by a charming living room that led into another kitchen. Everything was brown with sprinkles of red and yellow here and there. It felt like a cozy winter cabin.

In all the madness, I had forgotten I was supposed to call Halmoni when I got to safety.

I reached into my bag and pulled out my phone. After scrolling through the contacts, I pressed Halmoni's number.

It rang once and she picked up. "Lia?"

"Hi, Halmoni."

"Why didn't you call me earlier? Agent Kim's not picking up." She sounded worried.

I paused. "We met Agent Kim, but he didn't make it. Gaya got to him, too."

"Oh no. That's horrible. I can't believe he didn't make it. He was such a great agent." She paused for a moment, and then spoke in a choked voice. "Are you guys okay? Where are you?"

"Don't worry. We're okay now and at the family safe house."

"That's good." Then her voice turned serious and she spoke slowly. "But, Lia, if you're there, then that means it's time for plan C."

My parents really had thought of everything. Why was I not surprised?

"What is plan C?"

"It's for if you were ever left on your own."

"So do you know what I need to do?"

She paused before answering. "All they told me was that if it ever came to it, you should find something that was yours."

How mysterious. Find something of mine. I was pretty sure I'd never been here before. I wondered how anything of mine could've ended up here. Unless they made a trip here without me to set everything up. That must've been how they did this. It was so something they would do.

"And then what?"

"After that, I don't know," she said. "But whenever it was that they planned, they had no way of knowing how outpowered we'd be. Or just how dangerous things would get."

What was she trying to tell me? "Did something happen?"

"All the top agents are missing, dead, or unreachable."

That sounded very bad. And that meant no one was looking for my parents.

"Whatever it was that your parents wanted you to do, I can't let you go by yourself. You need to wait for me to get there."

I didn't want to argue, but she was injured badly, and I couldn't risk her getting hurt again.

"When are you going to get here?"

She coughed and cleared her throat. "I should be better in a few days. Just wait for me there."

That was a death sentence for my parents. Umma and Appa needed my help now. Today. Not three or four days from now. I wasn't going to sit around and wait for something to happen to them. Every second was precious.

I swallowed hard and decided it was better if I just agreed with her for now to put her mind at ease as she recovered. "Okay, Halmoni."

She blew a kiss over the phone. "I love you so much."

"I love you too." I turned to check if Joon was looking before I kissed her back.

The minute I hung up the phone, he walked toward me. "So what did she say?"

I debated whether to tell him the truth, but in the end this was a team effort. We needed to work together.

"She wanted us to wait a few days for her."

He thought for a minute, and then said, "But you don't want to?"

I nodded.

"I get it. If it were my parents, I'd want to find them right away too."

It felt good to know that Joon understood me and would stand by my decision. "I'd do anything to see them again."

He patted my back. "Well, if we were to find the jewel and rescue your parents, I bet IMA would have to accept both of us."

I almost chuckled. It was so like him to find something good even though we were so out of our league. Though I had to admit it was a brilliant idea. "That's true. They'd have to if we can do something that all the other agents failed at."

He smiled and rubbed his hands together. "It's the perfect plan to get us both in. They won't be able to say no to the duo who saved the day."

Sorry, Halmoni. I was going to follow plan C now.

But I'd leave my phone on so that she could find me. I didn't want her to worry. And besides, even if she wanted to, she wouldn't be able to come find us right away because of her injuries.

"Halmoni said the first thing to do is to find something that's mine."

Joon tilted his head and said, "Well, that shouldn't be too hard."

Did he not hear what I just said? "Are you serious? We have to search the entire place."

He shook his head and smiled. "I know the shortcuts for everything."

"What do you mean?"

"Come on." He walked past the kitchen and said, "Do you really think any of those pots and pans are yours?"

That was true. I loved food but didn't cook at all. Maybe the most I made at home was a sandwich or bagel.

He walked down the hallway and peeked into the first bedroom, with gray walls and a large bed. "Or those large textbooks and old movies?"

Then he walked into the second bedroom, with pink walls and toys on the shelves. "But this is clearly a kid's room. I bet that it's in here somewhere."

As annoying as he could be sometimes, he was totally right about this. Something of mine would have to be clothes, toys, books, or shoes.

The room was pretty bare and had a closet, a bed, and

a chest of drawers. I made a beeline for the closet and opened the door. It smelled musty and was completely empty. What kind of safe house had no clothes? I tapped on the four corners of the back of the closet, but nothing happened. I sighed, walked over to the chest, and opened all four drawers. All of them were empty. I felt along the back of the chest, but it was smooth and there was nothing hidden there.

My eye caught on the stuffed animals propped up against the pillows on the bed. A random assortment of a bunny, a teddy bear, an elephant, a pig, a monkey, and a kitten. Nothing looked familiar.

Wait. That monkey. It couldn't be.

I picked up the monkey, whose fur was matted. The smile was just as crooked as I remembered. The stuffing in one arm was almost gone because there was a hole, and I'd pulled it out. I looked closely at the arm and saw the black stitching that Umma had used to fix it. I lifted the monkey to my nose and inhaled. The smell of home brought a smile to my face. I had been devastated when I lost it. But my parents must've brought it here instead.

I looked behind me to make sure Joon wasn't looking and gave the monkey a big hug. Something sharp poked at my chest.

There was something sewn inside the monkey's chest.

"We need scissors," I said.

It pained me to cut open my beloved stuffed animal, but it had to be done.

Joon returned quickly with a pair of scissors. "What did you find?"

I held up the monkey. "I'm pretty sure this is it."

He laughed. "Okay, sure."

I had to be right or I'd never live this down. Using the scissors, I sliced the monkey's belly and spread it open.

"Look!" Inside was a black box with a yellow dragon delicately inlaid on top. The dragon, made of a shell-like material, had a long wavy body almost like a snake's. It had horns, four legs, a long beard, and had three claws on each foot. The dragon held a white pearl-looking ball in its mouth. Three-clawed dragons in Korea were a symbol for royalty. Not sure how that was important to me, but this was definitely it.

I took the box out and lifted the metal tab on the side that opened it.

Inside was a folded white paper.

That was it? What a letdown. I had hoped it was the jewel or some magical weapon to help save my parents.

"Well, hurry up and read it."

I opened the paper and read what was written out loud. "'Haeundae Matjib number two.'"

This was definitely a location. Even though I'd never been to Korea, I knew about Haeundae. It was a famous beach in Busan. And lucky for us, we were in Busan.

"I guess this means a trip to the beach tomorrow?"

I nodded. "But we don't know what 'Matjib number two' means."

Joon laughed. "Are you being funny? You, Miss Foodie, don't know what matjib is?"

My face turned red. "Oh, stop it."

"It literally means 'delicious house.' Slang for 'yummy restaurant.'"

"I see," I said quickly. There were so many shortened slang words in Korean, it was hard to keep up.

"I guess we can ask around for the second most popular restaurant tomorrow."

"Or maybe the place is actually called Second Best Restaurant."

"I doubt it. Want to bet on it?" He looked smug.

"Whoever wins will be known as Winner of the Year."

He laughed. "It's May already. But I'll enjoy you calling me that for seven more months."

CHAPTER 11

The next day, after a late breakfast, we made our way to Haeundae. It was within walking distance from the safe house.

"So where should we start?" Joon said as he stopped in front of a street lined with shops and restaurants.

I scanned the area and spotted a couple with linked arms walking by. "Watch and learn." I ran after them and tapped the woman's shoulder. "Excuse me."

Joon interrupted me before I could even speak. "Do you know where the second most delicious restaurant is?"

The woman shook her head. "Sorry. Don't know."

"How about a restaurant called Second Best? Something like that?" I asked.

"Oh, that one is pretty famous," she said. "It's called Second Best Restaurant, and they serve the most delicious abalone porridge."

I was right! "Where is it?"

She pointed down the street. "It's the fifth restaurant."

I bowed my head in thanks and watched them walk off.

Joon was already speed-walking to the restaurant.

"Wait for Winner of the Year," I yelled.

By the time I caught up to him, he was already standing in front of the restaurant. It was a little after eleven but bustling with people.

"Are you sure this is the right place?"

I opened the glass door. "Only one way to find out."

Inside, the savory smells from the kitchen filled the room. I had just eaten, but my mouth watered. One area had tables and chairs, while another section had traditional Korean seating on a little platform with low tables. Everyone there took off their shoes before stepping onto the platform and sitting on floor cushions.

A young man in an apron at the front desk greeted us. "How many people?"

"We're here from IMA," Joon announced.

I nudged Joon. He shouldn't be saying things like that in public. What was he thinking?

The man looked at Joon with a confused face. "Is that like NIS?"

NIS was the National Intelligence Service in Korea, similar to the CIA.

"Sorry, my friend didn't mean that," I said. "Can we speak to the owner?"

He nodded and yelled out, "Sajangnim!" Then he pointed for us to wait by the chairs near the front door. A young family walked past us and was guided to a table.

An elderly man with graying hair and a cane walked toward us from the back of the restaurant. He was dressed quite fashionably in a three-piece gray suit with a colorful tie.

"So how can I help you?" His eyes twinkled a bit as he looked at me.

I decided to tell him the truth. "My parents, Chung Mira and Park Minwoo, sent me here." In Korea, women kept their maiden name after they got married.

He smiled immediately at hearing their names. "It's been so long. How are they? You must be Lia."

My voice choked up, but I managed to say, "Well, that's why we're here."

He nodded gravely and motioned for us to follow him.

"Yes, yes. Only reason you'd be here was if they were in trouble."

We followed him past the tables and into the kitchen. There was so much steam coming from all the pots on the stove. He pulled open a large metal freezer door. I was thankful this was a seafood restaurant and there were no dead pigs hanging from the ceiling. In fact, there wasn't all that much in the freezer except for some buckets of ice.

"We make everything fresh and close the store when we use up all our ingredients."

No wonder everyone flocked here to eat. The food probably tasted amazing.

"Stand back." He turned the brass tiger perched on his cane ninety degrees clockwise. A large metal shelf glided aside, revealing a secret entrance that definitely wasn't there before.

I wanted to shout and clap, but I held it in.

He took out a large key from his pocket and fiddled with the lock.

"This, my friends, is the Premier Vault of Secrets." He opened the door to reveal rows and rows of safety-deposit boxes. They were stacked up to the ceiling. Red lasers crisscrossed the room. I felt like I was in a scene from a heist movie.

"We use a mixture of normal-people tech and magic."

It was pretty genius to hide a place like this in plain sight. The beefed-up security measures were also very impressive.

He snapped his fingers twice, and all the lasers powered off.

"Now, let me see where your box is."

In the middle of the room sat a large wooden cabinet with little drawers. He ran his fingers up and down until he stopped at one particular drawer.

The tiger on the cane opened its mouth. He raised it up, and the tiger's mouth clamped down on the handle, pulling the drawer out.

I peered inside, curious to see how they documented and recorded everything.

Paper. Lots and lots of index cards stacked up against each other.

"How do you find anything in here?" Joon asked.

"I'm guessing you two are too young to remember things like this. We use a card catalogue to store all our clients' information, but it can only be opened with magic." He chuckled and flipped through the cards until he found the right one.

He took glasses from his shirt pocket and put them on.

"There we go. Your box is way up there. Number 398."

"Uh. How do I get to it?"

He winked at me and said, "Just call out for it."

Joon giggled next to me. "Come down, box. Come down."

"Young man, this is no joking matter. Several wrong codes, and this place will go under lockdown."

"Sorry." He nudged me to go forward.

I took a deep breath and said, "Number 398."

There was a loud clanking of metal and the rows of boxes started moving, as if they were on a massive conveyor belt. After a couple seconds, a box slipped out in a row next to me. And then everything stopped.

"Well, there it is." He pointed to the door at the back of the room. "When you're done, exit through there."

"Thank you."

He nodded and walked away.

Joon pulled the box out and brought it over to a table near the card catalogue. It was made of metal, probably so it could be fireproof.

"Hurry, open it." He slid the box over to me.

I pulled the lid off. Inside was a metallic black rectangular object.

"Is that what I think it is?"

"Yeah. It's an older version, but it's an encrypted video message." My parents must've recorded this a few years ago. Or maybe even way before that.

"I've never seen one this old before." Joon looked at it more closely.

"Well, they say the older ones are actually more secure." I couldn't remember the reason why and hoped he wouldn't ask me.

I pressed my index finger down on the flat surface, and within three seconds the object whirred.

"You have to raise the recorder to your eye and look into the lens."

"I know, Joon."

I did as instructed, and just like a projector, a video clip of my parents flashed into the air. Umma had long hair here and looked younger. Appa had less gray in his hair and wasn't wearing glasses.

"Tap on the recorder to play it," Joon whispered.

I took a deep breath and gently pressed play.

"My darling daughter, Lia." Umma paused and awkwardly waved hi before continuing. "We hoped you would never find this. But if you are watching this now, please understand that we never meant to lie to you. From this point on, you need to forget everything we ever told you about magic. You need to learn magic and grow stronger. You are our daughter, and we know how powerful you can be. Remember what we used to do on your birthdays? That's how you're going to find the jewel. But whatever you do, you must get to the jewel before Gaya and destroy it. Do not under any circumstances give her the jewel. Even if it means you won't see us again. I know, baby. Don't cry. We wish it weren't this way too. Your one mission is to find and destroy the jewel. We love you so much and are so proud of you for being brave and making it here."

My hands trembled, and I rubbed my chest to ease the tightened muscles. I missed them so much, and even though they weren't actually here, it meant so much to see their faces and hear their voices.

I pressed play and watched it again.

And again.

I wasn't sure I could do this without them. I knew nothing about my new powers, and I really needed them to teach me and guide me. I guess I did have Umma's journal, but it wasn't the same thing. What made them think I'd be up for a mission? All I ever wanted to be was an agent and go on assignments and save the world, but I never thought I'd be doing it to save my own parents.

Joon stopped me from playing the video again and showed me the rest of the contents of the safety-deposit box.

All that was left was a piece of paper. Joon handed it to me. "Here. You do the honors."

I slowly opened the paper and read it out loud. "'What we loved doing in our backyard / Under / < What you think of Umma's special vase > .'"

"Do you know what it means?"

"This is our secret code. Every year on my birthday, my parents hid clues for my treasure hunt in different locations, eventually leading to my present. Each clue has three parts. The first part is the sentence right before the slash. And it always has to do with a place or object." I pointed to the word between the slashes. "This second section tells you where to look once you get there."

"And the last bit?" He pointed to the sentence inside the angle brackets.

"That's in case the location is too broad. It helps narrow it down. Or tells you what to do once you get there."

Joon put the lid back on the box. "Come on, let's get out of here."

Once we were outside, the weather had warmed up a little. I hadn't noticed before in our rush to find the restaurant, but a traveling carnival must've set up camp a block down. I saw a large Ferris wheel and a Viking ship ride. I had such good memories of going to carnivals with my parents and winning different prizes.

Joon must've read my mind, because he grabbed my arm and pulled me in the direction of the carnival. "Let's check that out," he said.

"I don't know." I wanted to, but at the same time, I felt guilty about having fun while my parents were who knew where.

"We can just clear our heads for a little bit. Figure out the clue."

"Okay. Just one ride." Maybe it would help us refocus and think. Come up with a plan.

We walked down the block and came upon the entrance of the carnival. I searched for a ticket booth and saw one a little farther in next to a game booth.

I ran toward the ticket booth. "Come on! This one's on me!"

"Okay, Winner of the Year," Joon said.

I smiled as I handed the attendant five thousand won in exchange for two tickets.

I turned to Joon and held them up in the air. "To the Ferris wheel!"

Joon groaned. "Lia, that's so boring. Only kids go on that."

I shrugged and gave my best pretend-sad face. "Winner of the Year gets to pick. And I pick the Ferris wheel."

He grumbled and walked toward the ride. "The Viking ship ride would've been my pick."

Thankfully, there was no line. We'd be in and out, just like that. This was only a teeny, tiny detour.

Because it had rained last night, the seats were a little wet. Joon took off his jacket and wiped my seat and his.

"Thanks, but that's so gross."

He shrugged. "It's just on the bottom. Do you want to get your pants wet?"

I quickly climbed in and sat down. "Ah. Nice and dry."

As he walked in, I pointed to a puddle on the floor. "Watch out!"

He stepped around it and sat down across from me.

I gazed out the window at the sparkling blue ocean. It really looked so beautiful from a distance. As long as I didn't have to go anywhere near it.

A few minutes later, the ride began to move. Joon took out his phone and pressed up closer to the window to take pictures.

I rubbed my arms to keep warm. That was strange.

It was a lot colder in this little compartment than it was outside.

Just then, all the water droplets started moving toward the middle of the floor. The puddle grew and grew.

I shrieked and lifted my feet up. "Joon!"

He turned back around to face me and said in an annoyed voice, "Shhhh. I'm taking a video."

"Look at the floor!" I pointed at the puddle, which was now almost reaching his sneakers.

He jerked his foot back. "What is that?"

We reached the top of the Ferris wheel, and all of a sudden, the ride stopped.

A voice on the speakers called out, "We're facing some technical difficulties. We will get the ride up and running in no time. Please stay calm."

"This is bad," I yelled as I lifted both my legs up onto my seat.

By now the water had covered the entire floor.

It continued to rise.

Joon held out his arm. "Try to get up and come on this side."

The hairs on my arms stood up. A strange force held my body down, and no matter how hard I tried, I couldn't move. "I can't."

He struggled in his seat. "Me either. It must be some sort of spell."

The water below us bubbled and swirled violently.

I sat frozen, mesmerized and terrified at the same time.

The water stopped spinning and a faint oval shape appeared. Then eyes, a nose, and a mouth formed inside the oval.

I shrieked.

Beads of sweat dripped down my forehead. The face grew hair and a neck. In a matter of seconds the image focused, and a beautiful and enchanting face stared back at me. She had thick black eyebrows, high cheekbones, a dainty nose, and full red lips. But the scariest part about her were her eyes. They were just completely black, even the part where the whites of the eyes should've been.

I grimaced and wanted to look away but couldn't. It was like the face was drawing me in toward it. My lips trembled and I squeezed my eyes shut.

The face spoke in a slow, high-pitched voice. "Lia. We meet at last."

"Who are you?" I squeaked.

I couldn't believe there was a face in the water and I was talking to it. All I wanted was to clear my head.

She giggled and said, "Sweet girl. I'm Gaya."

Oh my gosh. This was Gaya? This scary, evil person seemed too pretty. Her laugh was almost musical. Not at all what I imagined a monster who'd kidnap my parents would look like. If you took out her freaky appearance in a pool of water on a Ferris wheel, she was just another good-looking lady.

"What do you want?" I barked back.

"I trust you got my message," she said as she glared at me. "Just a tiny, little jewel."

"Let me see my parents." I needed to stand my ground and make sure they were okay.

She disappeared for a second, and I saw an image of my parents with cuffs on their hands and feet, huddled on the floor in a dark room. "You see? They are alive and well. For now."

Seeing them was not reassuring at all. But at least I didn't see any bleeding or signs that they had been tortured.

Then she appeared again. "I hate repeating myself." Her eyes narrowed and she pursed her lips. "Bring me the jewel, and in return I'll give you back your parents."

There was so much hatred in her eyes, enough to burn a hole right through me. But I refused to back down. I needed to negotiate. "If I bring you the jewel, I want them alive."

"Yes. I promise they will be alive. You give me what I want. I will return them to you in one piece."

"Now's probably not a good time to tell you this. But I really have no idea what jewel you're talking about."

Her face turned paler as her eyes grew larger and darker. "The dragon's jewel." She turned to the side and said, "You didn't tell her?" in a scathing voice.

I heard muffled sobs and knew she was threatening my parents. "It's not their fault! I'll get it for you!"

"You most definitely will," she said with a sneer.

"Just tell me," I demanded. "Where is the jewel?"

"Oh, my little Hwarang. If I knew that, why would I need you?" She cackled and then disappeared.

Just as fast as the water grew, it subsided, and all the droplets went back to where they were before. The Ferris wheel jerked and started to move again.

The force keeping me frozen disappeared. I lifted my leg up. "I can move again."

Joon wiggled both legs. "Me too."

We just stared at each other, unable to form words.

CHAPTER 12

When we got back to the safe house, we silently ate the samgak kimbap that I had bought yesterday. "Just telling you now, I don't care what they said in the video. I'm not going to let my parents die."

"Yeah. I get it." He had a wistful look on his face. "But they specifically said not to give Gaya the jewel. . . ."

"I know. But come on," I said. "It's not like we ever believed that Gaya would keep her word and set my parents free even if we gave her the jewel."

"Good point," he said. "We can't trust her."

"What's so special about the jewel, anyway?" I wondered.

He shrugged. "No idea. No one knows much about it except that it's super powerful."

"Ugh. That is so not helpful."

"Sorry. You're the Hwarang. It's technically your job to know all this stuff."

I ignored his comment. I wished I knew about all this too and that my parents hadn't been taken hostage by some power-hungry lady who wanted a jewel. But I was just learning about myself and my lineage, so he really needed to be quiet and cut me some slack.

I took out the clue from my pocket and read it again.

"So where is it?"

"I'm not sure. But we used to love camping in our backyard and looking up at the stars."

Joon whipped out his phone, pressed a button, and placed it on the floor. A search engine popped up into the air. He touched it and a keyboard appeared below the screen. "Okay. I'm going to skip camping. There are too many camping grounds."

"Maybe a place to see stars, then?" I suggested.

He typed *observatory* on the keyboard. "Still too broad," he said. "What's the third hint?"

"I used to say that the vase looked ugly and old." I wish I had said nicer things to my mom. She really treasured that vase, which was now broken.

He chuckled. "I'm going to go with old."

A list of places and images showed up on the screen. Joon tapped on the first image of an old run-down building. He swiped left.

The next image was of a newer building in Seoul.

"Let's just see all the images first," I said.

Joon nodded and swiped his hand left.

My eyes glazed over the images of observatories, which all looked similar to each other. They had definitely all been built within the last hundred years.

"Wait. Go back."

He swiped right and stopped on the image of a strange brick structure that looked almost like a chimney.

"What is that?" I asked.

"That's an observatory called Cheomseongdae."

I remembered this from IMA class. "Built during the Silla dynasty, right?"

He scrolled down to read the description. "Yeah. You're right."

"That's got to be the old one my parents are talking about."

"Let me check." He moved his index fingers diagonally across the screen and enlarged the text.

"See, there. It says it was built in the seventh century and is the oldest astronomical tower in the world."

"Location down!" He raised his hand and I slapped him a high five. Small victories.

"So where is this place?"

He tapped on a link and a map filled the screen. "Cheomseongdae was built in Seorabeol, the capital of the Silla dynasty, which was known for its advanced understanding of science and math."

"And that's right there." I pointed to a part of the map. "Seorabeol is modern-day Gyeongju."

I couldn't stop beaming. We'd cracked a part of the puzzle already.

"We can check it out tomorrow."

"It doesn't seem too far from here." I stretched my arms and yawned.

As Joon leaned over to search for a few books, I caught a glimpse of his birthmark. It was the shape of maybe half a circle. I focused my eyes and saw what looked to be an eyebrow, an eye, part of a nose, and half of a mouth. It was half of a smiling face, which looked a bit mysterious.

He noticed I was staring and quickly sat up.

"Sorry. I didn't mean to look."

He pulled down his shirt slightly to reveal the birthmark a little below his collarbone. "It's strange, isn't it?"

"It's unique. I've never seen anything like it."

"My mom said I've had it all my life."

"Maybe it's genetic. Do your parents have one too? I know I have a mole on my foot, and so does my mom."

He shook his head and paused for a moment. "No. They don't."

I gasped in excitement. "I know! Maybe it's a symbol or a sign. Like a mark that means you're the chosen one."

He laughed. "You really watch too many movies. And besides, between the two of us, all signs point to you being the chosen one."

"What did your parents say when you called them at Halmoni's house?" I realized I had never asked him.

"Dad is actually leading the task force to try and find Gaya from back home." He paused before adding, "And they think I'm still with your grandma."

"Shouldn't you call them again?" I still felt bad keeping him here with me. I knew we made a pact to do this together, but the stakes kept getting higher. If he could go back home to his parents where he'd be safe, he should.

"And miss out on this?" He grinned. "You should

know better than anybody how boring our town is."

Thank goodness he still felt the same way.

Maybe I could help him figure out if the birthmark meant anything. My detective skills were top-notch. I reached out my hand and said, "Can I see it again?"

Joon jolted up and speed-walked to the bathroom. "I'm going to wash up. Good night."

I drew my hand back and tucked my hair behind my ears. "Okay. Good night." Darn it. Me and my big mouth. I must've said something wrong. I walked to the room with stuffed animals and plopped down on the bed. I was too tired to wash my face. All I wanted to do was snuggle under the blanket and sleep.

CHAPTER 13

"Wake up! Wake up!" Joon barged through the door and switched on the lights.

I squinted and covered my eyes with my hands. "Oh my gosh. What are you doing?"

"Time to get up!" He opened the shades.

"Are you serious? It's too early." I groaned and smooshed my face into the pillow. "Go away. I'm going back to sleep."

Joon plopped down on the bed and tugged at my blanket. "Stop being such a baby. Get up."

I held on tight and muttered, "What's the big deal?"

"We have to get there before the tourists start coming," he said in an exasperated tone. Last night, we were about to figure out a time to leave, before Joon walked off all of a sudden. And he wasn't even apologizing for it right now. An *I'm sorry about running off last night* would make me feel better.

"Okay," I said. "Can you get out of my room so I can change, please?"

He hopped off the bed and said, "Going. Five minutes!"

The door shut behind him. I stretched my arms and legs as long as I could. Probably grew an inch. Another day, another treasure hunt. Normally, I'd love chasing clues, but not with my parents' lives at stake.

I slid off the bed and walked to the bathroom. This safe house didn't have much everyday stuff, but at least there was toilet paper and a bar of soap. I turned on the water and splashed my face. The cool water dripping down my cheeks woke me up instantly. Using a couple pieces of toilet paper, I dabbed my face dry. I ran my fingers through my hair to untangle it and tied it up in a ponytail. I pressed my hands down against the sink and looked at my reflection.

This is a new day. Today you will find your parents. You got this.

I pumped my arms a couple times. This self-coaching

always gave me a bit more confidence. I needed every ounce of it today.

I walked out to the kitchen to find Joon sitting at the table, looking at one of the books.

He looked up and chuckled. "There you are, sleepy-head. Ready?"

Maybe I was just overreacting to this whole thing. Seemed like he was back to his usual self, so I guessed it was no big deal. I smiled extra big and said, "Sure. Let's go."

Once we were outside, I tugged on the door to make sure it was locked. Old habits. Back home, whoever was the last one out had to check the door.

The streets were empty except for a couple cars driving by. I hated being up this early. My body felt like it was going to curl up in a ball and fall asleep.

Joon took a big whiff of air and stretched his arms. "It's a new day!"

Gosh. He was so annoyingly cheery. No question in my mind he was a morning person.

He pulled out his phone. "Low battery. Can you enter the address on yours?"

Of course I could, now that I had this cool smartphone.

But just like Joon, I had forgotten to charge it. I only had maybe 10 percent battery left, and I should keep it on for Halmoni in case she got worried. "I don't have much left either."

"So which way, then?" he asked.

I pulled out a ripped page from my pocket. "Found a tourist map of Gyeongju in one of the books in the living room yesterday."

Joon struggled to hold in his laughter. "You're just like your mom."

I didn't know whether to be happy or sad about that.

But I ignored him and continued. "That's a strange place to hide a jewel, don't you think?" It didn't make sense to me for something to be hidden in a spot where there were so many people visiting every day. But maybe that was the point. Hidden in plain sight, like the Premier Vault of Secrets.

He shrugged. "I'm sure your parents had a plan."

I pointed to a spot on the map I had circled last night. "This is where we need to go."

A bus pulled to a stop up ahead. "That's our bus," I said. "Come on!"

We waved our arms and jumped out into the street,

hoping the driver would see us and wait. He left the door open and we hopped on.

Joon bowed his head and said, "Thank you," while placing his phone against the reader.

"You know, I should really pay you back for everything," I called after him. The bus jerked to a start, and my body lurched forward.

Joon held my arm and steadied my balance. "Or I should pay you back. The KTX train tickets were way more expensive."

I nodded and scooted into my seat. "You're going to have a big bill by the time we get back home."

He laughed. "Don't worry. I'm good for it."

I yawned and leaned my head against the window.

"Sleepyhead. You can go back to sleep now. It's going to be over an hour until we get there."

I chuckled and closed my eyes. "Don't mind if I do."

"I'll wake you up if you snore."

I rolled my eyes but couldn't help smiling. A ten-minute power nap and then I'd be good—

A searing pain shot through my head. I groaned and rubbed my temples.

"Are you okay?" Joon peered over with a concerned look on his face.

"Yeah. I'll be fine. I've been having these horrible headaches since we got to Busan."

"We can get some medicine later if you want."

"It's okay. I'm probably just overtired or something." I closed my eyes and cringed in pain.

But this time a chill ran up my spine as a memory I didn't know I had flashed before my eyes. I had been here before. In this very city.

Waves lapped against a large white boat, rocking it rhythmically back and forth.

"Up, up!" I squealed. Appa scooped me up and placed me on his lap. He wrapped his arms around me like a pretend seat belt and made a clicking noise as he clasped his hands together. I giggled and pressed my head back into his chest. Appa always knew how to make me laugh.

"Look, Appa!" I pointed at the sun hitting the ocean, and Appa held me tighter than he ever had before. A dark stream of smoke billowed up from the treetops by the shore. At first, it looked like the tree was on fire, except there were no flames.

Umma jumped up and quickly walked to the other side of the boat to get a closer look. But the boat drifted farther away from the shore. The smoke rose up into the sky and did something no smoke should do: it changed directions and dived into the water. She stood on the ledge of the railing and looked down into the water. I squirmed out of Appa's arms and ran over to see what Umma was looking at.

"Lia, no!" Appa chased after me. But I ignored him because I was too busy staring at the fish scattering to the right and left, as if they were running away from something bigger and scarier.

Appa reached for my hand and Umma lunged at me, but they were too late. Two watery arms stretched out from the ocean and lurched at me. "Umma!" I screamed and wailed as the arms wrapped around my waist and dragged me into the ocean. I couldn't breathe.

When I looked up, I saw the bottom of the boat and Umma diving into the water after me. I reached out to her but the arms pulled me deeper into the water.

Umma mouthed something, but I couldn't understand what she was saying. Or if she was even talking to me. She stretched out her arms, and I saw her repeat something over and over again. I tried to turn around to look at what was holding me, but the grip around me was too tight, and I couldn't move. Sparks flew and the watery arms wrapped around me grew hard and froze like a statue, and then completely disintegrated into ash. Umma grabbed me, holding me tight in her arms, and kicked as fast as she could until we reached the surface.

Appa threw down a rope, and Umma cradled me in one arm and used the other hand to tie the rope around her waist. After pulling us up to safety, Appa asked, "Is she breathing?"

Umma pressed her ear against my mouth and nodded. Her hot tears dripped onto my skin as she caressed my face. I didn't understand what she said next. But she said it with such intensity that it drove fear into my heart.

"It was her. It had to be her. She knows," said Umma.

Joon shook my shoulders. "Hey, are you okay?"

I opened my eyes and saw that we were still on the bus.

He handed me a tissue from his pocket. "You were crying. What's going on?"

I'd never been so relieved to see him. How could I explain what I'd just seen? Was it even real? "I don't know." I hugged him and just wept.

He patted my back and said, "You're okay now. I'm here if you want to talk."

I took a deep breath and wiped my face. "I think I remembered something from my past."

"What do you mean? Did you lose your memories?"

"I didn't think I did. But now that I think about it, I don't remember anything from my life before moving to California. I always thought it was because I was too little to remember. But now, I'm not so sure."

"Nothing at all?"

"Nope."

"What about pictures?"

"My parents said we lost a box of old pictures on the move here."

He snapped his fingers. "I got it. Maybe they also put a memory-blocking spell on you."

But that didn't make any sense. What could've been so bad about my childhood that they had to keep me from remembering it? And then it hit me. Everything clicked. Both the magic and the memory blockers were for my protection. Maybe Gaya had been after me my whole life and my parents had been trying to shield me from it all.

"They were trying to keep me safe."

But then why were the memories coming back? My hands grew cold as an awful thought entered my head. "Do you think it's because something's happened to my parents?"

He thought for a moment. "Doubt it. Even death wouldn't undo a strong spell."

I tried to remember what my parents said in the video message, to forget everything they'd told me and embrace who I was. "Maybe this is part of their plan. Only the spell caster can undo it, right?"

My parents wanted me to remember.

CHAPTER 14

The bus stopped in front of a small grove of trees.

"This is our stop," Joon said.

We got off and walked past an empty admissions booth and a closed gate. Joon stuck his foot in a gap in the gate and tried to climb it.

I looked around and saw a red light blinking back at me from the corner of the ticket booth. "Wait." I pointed up. "Look. There are security cameras everywhere."

"Darn. We need to find another way in." He took his hands off the gate and walked to me.

I took a few steps back and spotted a stone wall surrounding the entire outdoor park. I raced to the left past the ticket booth, around a corner, and into an alley.

The entire wall was made of rocks with a little tiled roof at the very top. It wasn't very high, either. I yelled for Joon to come over.

I'd found a way in.

"Ready to climb?" I asked.

He chuckled. "You are talking to the master rock climber."

"Race you, then." There was no way I was going to let him win.

We both placed our hands on the rocks and said, "One, two, three!"

I grabbed the edges of the stones and jammed my feet into the crevices of the wall. It took a couple minutes, but I scaled the wall with relative ease and hopped over.

Joon grunted and I heard an occasional "ow" as he climbed.

"I'm waiting."

He jumped down. "It's because you're smaller than me."

"Excuses, excuses." I laughed and patted his back. "It's okay. You know you didn't really stand a chance anyway." I always beat him when we went rock climbing at the gym back home.

"Because you're lighter than me."

I waved peace signs with both my hands. "Don't be jealous of my skills. Just call me Winner of the Year, please."

"You're so annoying sometimes, Lia," Joon said as he marched ahead of me.

Instead of trees and benches, large hilly mounds surrounded the entire area. It looked like grassy sand dunes everywhere.

"Are you sure we're in the right place?" Joon asked.

I took out the map and showed him. "See, almost there. We have to go through this area first."

"What kind of park is this?" asked Joon. "I sort of remember learning about this."

"It's not a park with a playground. This is Daereungwon. The Royal Tomb Complex."

He had his magic powers to fall back on, so I doubt he had memorized as many facts as I had. I needed all the points I could get on the multiple-choice section.

I couldn't believe we were standing in the middle of a cemetery. It didn't seem as creepy as walking through a graveyard, even though it pretty much was. To my surprise, it actually looked beautiful and serene. I felt my heart beat a little slower and my tensed-up shoulders begin to relax.

"This is where all the kings and queens from the Silla dynasty are buried," I said.

"Oh, that's right," Joon said as he walked next to me.

"Only Cheonmachong Tomb is open to the public," I said. "It's named after a painting of a cheonma, a mystical Korean horse with eight legs and wings on its feet."

Up ahead I saw a large sign that pointed right and read *Cheomseongdae*. I almost jumped up and down in excitement.

Except scattered throughout the park were large white poles with security cameras placed at the top.

I pointed to the cameras, and Joon looked around and said, "Yeah. I noticed them too."

"We'll have to avoid them and take the long way there," I said.

Instead of taking the path marked on the map, we dodged the cameras and wove through a maze of trees, tombs, and mini pagodas—little gray structures that looked like ladies with skirts and hats on.

"We have to hurry. Come on!" Joon ran ahead with my map in his hand.

I followed close behind him until he stopped.

An old and unremarkable stone tower stood in front of us. It wasn't very tall, and there were no clear entryways.

Most of the structure was cylindrical except for the square top, which looked like a chimney. About halfway up there was a little cutout window.

"We made it." He put his hands on his legs and panted.

"It's designated as national treasure number thirty-one."

I was disappointed. It looked more run-down and smaller than the picture we'd seen back at the safe house.

"How are we supposed to open this thing?" He circled around the structure.

I pulled out the paper from my pocket and opened it. "It says 'under.' Maybe the next clue is on the ground somewhere."

As the words left my mouth, I realized how silly that sounded. This was an outdoor area with a lot of foot traffic. My very smart but meticulous parents wouldn't hide a clue somewhere that anyone walking by could just stumble upon. That much I knew.

Joon walked back to me and pointed at the cutout halfway up the tower. "I don't see any way in except for that."

"You think the clue could be inside?" I tilted my head and stared at the window.

"Not sure. But I didn't see anything under. Did you?"

"We just have to be smarter about looking. If my parents hid it inside, the clue would say 'inside' and not 'under.'"

He threw his hands in the air. "Okay, okay. You know your parents."

I knelt down and ran my hands across the grass. It felt wet from the morning dew. Maybe it was hidden in the grass. But then it could just get blown away by the wind. That wouldn't be a very smart way to hide something important.

"Check the bricks." Maybe the clue was in one of them. But there were so many. How were we going to find the right one?

"What am I looking for?" Joon asked, running around and touching each one.

I sighed. Sometimes he was just so useless. "I don't know. Something that seems off."

"I don't see anything," he yelled. "Come on. Let's just climb in."

"No. I'm sure it's here somewhere." I sat down on the grass. My parents wouldn't make it that simple.

I crouched down and examined the bottom row of bricks. They all seemed to be relatively the same size. I crawled around and poked each one. Joon joined in and started in the opposite direction.

I came across a slightly darker and smaller one than the rest. I tapped on it and felt it wiggle.

"Got something!"

Joon walked over and sat down next to me.

I pushed against one end of the brick and the other side popped out just a little. "Help me pull this out."

He grabbed the brick and yanked it out.

I stuck my hand inside and fished out a piece of paper.

"What does it say?"

I read out loud, "'Like your closet / In front / < Dokkaebi Bangmangi > .'"

"What does it mean? Do you get it?"

I waved my hand at him to be quiet so I could think. Like my closet? I had clothes in there. Some boxes. And then my secret IMA closet. That must be it!

Joon stood with his hands on his hips and stared up at the window. "I still think this is our best shot in."

"Will you just wait a second? I almost cracked it." Now for the second part. That was easy. Stand in front. And the third? Had no idea what that was about.

"What do you have so far?" Joon asked.

"Okay. So we are looking for a secret door, and it's

in front," I said. "The third part, I'm not sure."

"The last part seems kind of important, doesn't it?" Joon asked as he reread the clue. "What do you remember from 'Dokkaebi Bangmangi'?"

It was one of the many Korean folktales my parents used to read to me. This one was about a woodcutter who was gathering acorns for his family when he came across a group of dokkaebi, also known as goblins. He saw them do magic with a bangmangi, which was basically a magic club. The woodcutter got so hungry, he ate one acorn, and the noise scared the dokkaebi away. But they left behind the bangmangi, which he took home and used for good.

"You know what? There was a song. A special one that the dokkaebi sang when using the bangmangi," I said.

"Now that you brought it up, I can almost hear the tune in my head," Joon said.

I thought back for a moment and remembered that after reading the book, I would play a game with my parents. They'd hand me a rolled-up piece of newspaper, and I'd swing it around, pretending it was a magical bat. But my memories ended there.

"We need to hurry up. The tours are going to start soon," Joon said.

I really wanted to get inside, but where would I begin? Without the third part, it would be impossible to find the next clue. But maybe focusing on the first two parts would jog my memory. I stood in front of the structure, and no matter how hard I stared at it, no door appeared.

"Maybe you should use your magic," he whispered to me.

I stared at him. Was he joking? "Uh. Negative. No way." Clearly, I couldn't control my powers yet. What if I accidentally hurt him and he couldn't heal?

As if he knew what I was thinking Joon said, "You don't have to worry about injuring me."

I smiled weakly. But I still felt uneasy about using magic again. So much could go wrong.

"Just think about it, okay?" He paused and then added, "It's the only way if we want to save your parents."

Fair point. Then there was one other big reason I couldn't possibly use magic. "Didn't you hear Halmoni? If I do, the shadows will find me."

"So what? It's not like Gaya doesn't know what we're up to."

That was true. She pretty much gave me her blessing to go find this jewel. But the problem was I only knew two spells. Although there seemed to be a lot of variations to them. There wasn't enough time to learn a new one right now. I'd have to make do with the ones I knew.

"This was made for you. Only you can do it, and I'm sure your parents knew you'd be up to the task. They could've kept all this secret, but they didn't." Joon held my shoulders firmly and looked me in the eye. "I believe in you, Lia."

I couldn't help but laugh. He looked so serious. "Thanks for the pep talk."

Feeling encouraged, I inhaled the crisp morning air and pictured Umma and Appa in hopes of centering my thoughts. But I couldn't get the image of them bound up out of my head. I needed to find my happy place, because my heart was pounding against my chest and I couldn't concentrate. I thought about our Saturday family movie nights and how Umma let me put extra butter on my popcorn. My hands would get all greasy from the butter, and I would lick them while my parents fake-gasped in horror.

Here goes. I thought about moving bricks around to form a larger opening and chanted, "Idong." And just for good measure I added, "Umjigyeora."

Move, bricks. Move!

Nothing budged. I focused harder on the structure and chanted. A loud crumbling sound filled the air. The bricks from the top of the structure crashed to the ground one by one.

"Undo whatever you just did!"

I stopped chanting and the bricks stopped falling.

He looked at his watch. "It's eight forty-five! The park opens at nine. You need to think of something quick."

Maybe the entrance was hidden somewhere in the grass, like a trapdoor. I pictured the grass parting and chanted again, "Umjigyeora."

Move. Please move.

Joon gasped and shook my arm. "Look!"

The grass swayed as if blowing in the wind, except there wasn't even the slightest breeze today. I covered my mouth and stepped back to get a better look. The grass stopped moving.

"Keep doing what you just did. You can't stop."

I really hoped this was the right spell, but there was only one way to find out. "Umjigyeora."

"It's working again!" Joon yelled. "Keep going!"

As I chanted, the grass around the structure rustled until it began to part, revealing the soil underneath.

Joon ran over and sifted through the soil with his fingers. "There's nothing here."

"I need the last clue. I can't do it without it." I racked

my brain for the words to the childhood song about the magical bat.

"Is this it?" He hummed a tune.

"Got it!" I shouted. "Geum nawara ttukttak! Eun nawara ttukttak!"

Now I remembered. I had thought it was silly but oh so fun to dance and shout, "Gold, appear! Silver, appear!" Of course, I didn't have magic back then, so nothing happened.

I stood in front of the structure and pictured a door opening—just like my secret IMA closet door that disappeared—and chanted, "Geum nawara ttukttak! Eun nawara ttukttak!"

A row of bricks along the base floated out in front of me. Then another row on top of that. And then another.

I cringed and waited for the structure to collapse, but it stood firm.

Joon gasped and got down on the ground and peeked inside.

I continued to chant and jumped up and down. It was working.

I had done something right.

The bricks floated in midair, leaving a hole in the structure just big enough for us to slip through.

In the distance we heard whistles and a man shouting, "Hey! Get away from there!"

I turned around and saw a group of people and a police officer racing toward us. A man in glasses yelled, "Someone stop them! This tower is a national treasure."

There was only one thing to do now.

Go inside this hole. I needed to trust this was what my parents had intended to happen.

Joon went inside first. "Watch your step. There's a ladder here."

I took a deep breath and climbed down the ladder. It was so dark inside, I wasn't sure how deep it was. I just kept climbing down.

From below Joon yelled, "Shut the door! Shut it!"

Outside, the shouting and the whistles grew closer. I imagined the bricks closing again and whispered, "Umjigyeora." *Move. Please close.* This time I said it with a firmness and confidence that came with my last victory. The light began to disappear, and I heard the clacking sounds of the bricks moving again.

Only one way to go now. Down.

CHAPTER 15

I clung to the ladder. It was so dark, I couldn't see anything. Who knew how far this went down and what was waiting for us at the bottom? Could be anything.

I jammed my finger against the brick wall while reaching for the next rung and cried out in pain. I screamed as my arms flailed and I tumbled backward.

It was a short fall, and I landed with a thud on the floor. The wind got knocked out of me and everything blacked out.

I gasped for air as I woke up to Joon propping me up against a wall.

"Are you okay? You have to be more careful!"

I groaned and rubbed the back of my head. He was starting to sound like my parents. "I'm fine."

He bumped my shoulder as he sat down next to me. "I thought I lost you there. You're lucky you weren't too far from the ground when you fell."

I looked around but couldn't make out anything. "Where are we?"

"Don't know," he said. "But we're pretty much trapped down here."

That couldn't be right. My parents would never send me to a dead end.

We must have missed something.

I took out my phone, turned on the flashlight, and shined it around the room.

Stone walls surrounded us. We were in a rectangular hallway of sorts with nothing but a ladder to go back up and two torches. Something white stuck out from the bottom of the torch on the right.

I stood up and walked over to the wall with the torches.

Joon jolted up. "Did you find something?"

I pulled out a folded piece of paper jammed under the bottom of the torch on the right.

"This must be the next clue." I opened the paper and

read, "'What you're embarrassed to admit but you still use at night / Right and left / < Turn on >.'"

"Well, this one's easy. It's talking about the two torches," I said quickly.

My face turned red. I knew exactly what my parents were talking about. Every now and then I had nightmares, so I still used a night-light. Now that I thought about it, the night-lights I had at home were shaped just like the torches, with a rectangular plug and a fan-shaped top where the light shone through.

"So what's the thing you're embarrassed about?" Joon cocked his head and smiled.

"You don't need to know that. The last part of the clue is what to do. And the answer is light. The clue basically says to light the two torches."

He stood next to me and touched one of the torches. "Great. Go ahead and do it."

I laughed. What did he think I was, some magician and I could just snap my fingers and the lights would turn on?

Sometimes magic wasn't always the answer.

"Luckily for you, I'm always prepared." I reached inside my bag and grabbed my trusty little pouch, which I took with me wherever I went.

I dug around in my pouch until my fingers curled around the familiar square shape of my matchbook. These were hard to come by nowadays, but my parents had jars of matchbooks that they'd collected from restaurants back in the day.

"Here it is." I held it up so that Joon could see.

"Is that a matchbook?" He took it from my hand and flipped it open. "I've never seen one in real life before."

I took it back from him and pulled out a match. "Watch and learn. This is how I'm going to save the day."

"Do you even know how to use it?" He took a couple steps back.

I chuckled. "Don't worry. I've seen my parents use it to light candles." Time to get down to business. I placed the match on the black strip and closed the flap over it. The next part wasn't my favorite. I cringed, took a deep breath, and yanked the match out. It burst into flames.

I tipped the match so that the fire would touch the inside of the left torch. Nothing happened. I held the match there for a couple more seconds until the flame crept to my fingers. I shook it out.

"What the . . ." Joon touched the torch. "It's not even hot. Are you sure you held it close enough?"

"Of course I did." What an annoying question. As if I didn't know how to light something. "It's the torch that's broken."

"Here. Let me try." Joon took the matchbook from me.

"Be my guest." He would just have to find out the hard way, then.

"Maybe we need to light the torches in the order they're listed." He struck a match against the strip, and it burst into flames.

I held my breath as he held the match over the torch on the right. A part of me hoped it wouldn't work, because if it did, that would mean he was right about the clue.

"It's not working!" He flicked his hand to put the match out.

I crossed my arms in front of me and said in a smug voice, "I know. That's what I just said."

"Sorry. Just wanted to double-check." He flashed a sheepish half smile and sat down on the ground next to me.

I sat down on the ground and leaned my back against the wall. This might take a while. Why were the matches not lighting the torch? Logically, they should. It was the weirdest thing.

Maybe magic was the answer this time.

Joon sighed. "Like I said before, you need to use your magic."

Deep down I knew using magic was the only way out of this place. We could climb back up, but the police were probably waiting for us by now. Or we could wait it out until nightfall, but then we would lose an entire day. Who knew how patient Gaya would be? I couldn't risk something happening to my parents.

There was nothing down here except the two torches, which were obviously meant to be lit. I guessed we could figure out what to do after we could see better.

Joon poked my arm a couple times and handed me the matchbook. "Are you doing a spell?"

I placed it on the floor and said, "Shhh. Let me think."

How was I even going to create light? This seemed like very high-level magic. I doubted I'd leveled up that much.

I took out Umma's journal from my bag and handed Joon my phone. He clicked on the flashlight function and held it up as I flipped through the pages. There must be something in here to solve this.

A few pages in, I came across a spell called butigeora. Only catch was that butigeora meant to light or attach. I'd have to be very careful with this spell because I could end up with two very different results. According to Umma's notes, this spell channeled gi to ignite what was already intended to be lit. I think she meant that I couldn't use this spell to throw flaming light balls at villains as a superhero might. "This could work." I showed Joon the notes.

He held the book in his hands and nodded while reading. "Okay, I'll walk you through it. Picture what you want to light and then chant."

In my mind I imagined a large fire, like the flames of the campfire my parents and I would roast marshmallows around.

"Bul butigeora."

Please light up.

I felt a warmth near my legs and I opened my eyes. On the ground in between us, flames sparked one by one on each matchstick, growing bigger and bigger until it became one large flame. Of course, it had to be a magic flame that flitted across the ground.

Joon whipped off his jacket and flung it at the fire.

I huddled back near the wall and pointed to the left. "It's going that way! Catch it! Catch it!"

He held out his hand in front of me. "Stay back!" After a couple more intense moments of throwing his jacket down, the fire was out.

I rubbed my hands together and sighed. I wish I had better control of my powers. Who knew I could start a dancing flame? Even though it was in the wrong place, I had still turned on fire.

Joon panted and rested his back against the wall. "Maybe you should be more specific."

"Oh, are you the genius spellmaker now?"

His frustration annoyed me. I knew he just wanted to hurry up and find the jewel. I did too. But this new spell-making power was hard to control.

This time I pictured lighting the two torches in front of me, the right one first and then the left. "Bul butigeora." I squeezed my eyes shut and hoped that the torches were lit. There was a hissing sound, and I felt warmth on my face.

Joon patted my back. "You did it!"

My eyes widened when I saw the fire on both torches. I covered my mouth with my hands.

Dust fell on top of our heads. I huddled next to Joon, and we looked up. But it was hard to tell where the dust was coming from. I coughed and pounded my chest.

The bricks on the wall in front of us between the torches started moving. Some to the right, others to the left. Like curtains parting, except they were bricks.

I grabbed Joon's hand and pulled him back.

"Oh my gosh. Oh my gosh." I stood dumbfounded and at a loss for words. Definitely wasn't expecting this.

Soon the bricks had moved around to create a little archway for us.

A piece of white paper floated down. This must be another clue. I picked it up and stuffed it in my pocket. I'd read it later after we got past this.

Joon tapped the bricks. "It seems safe."

"This is crazy." I was hesitant to walk through. What if it collapsed on us? That was a very real possibility.

"Come on. Let's go." He ducked under the archway and disappeared.

"Wait for me." I took a deep breath and walked through behind him.

We entered a narrow hallway with torches lining the brick walls. Every time we got close to one, it would light up on its own. At the end of the hall was a wooden door.

Joon stood in front of the door, but nothing happened, even when he pushed on it. As I walked closer, it creaked open and started to lift up. He stared at me as if I had done something I shouldn't have.

"Did you use magic to open the door?"

"No. Not at all." Maybe he was just jealous that I'd gotten the door to open.

"Hmm. Interesting," he said.

"What do you mean?"

We waited for the door to lift up. It was the slowest-moving thing ever. "I think it's cool how your parents designed this whole place just for you."

"Yeah. I guess it is," I said. "Whatever this place is."

"I mean, even the door recognizes you and opens for you."

"Can doors even do that?"

"I'm sure it's a magic door," he said.

Apparently too impatient to wait, Joon crouched down and peeked under the slow-moving door. "You're not going to believe what's on the other side. Come on!"

I shuffled my body under the door, and Joon followed right behind me.

The entire room was lit with candles. From floor to ceiling, there were bookshelves filled with books. The ceiling was in a dome shape. But the most striking thing of all were the books floating in the air.

I smiled and jumped to try to catch one of them. As I reached up, the book floated away. "Oh my gosh. Did you see that?"

"This is unbelievable." Joon jumped too, trying to catch a book with both hands.

"I'm going to take a wild guess here and say this is a library," I said.

Joon chuckled. "The best library I've ever been to."

I walked over to the bookshelves and tried to pull out a book, but it wouldn't budge. I leaned back and pulled again with all my strength, but it wouldn't move. What was wrong with them? Maybe they were fake.

"These won't come out either." Joon stood at the other end of the room, yanking on the books.

We looked at each other and sighed.

I plopped down on the floor and opened my bag.

"Anything good in there?" His stomach growled.

I took out a bag of chips. "Want some?"

He opened it and grabbed a handful. We munched on the chips while admiring the floating books.

"Any ideas on how to get those books down?" asked Joon.

"Nope. But I bet it's in here." I flipped through Umma's journal again, but this time I couldn't find anything about how to deal with flying books.

Come on, Lia, think. If my parents designed this for me, they must've left a tool or an object that I could use.

I scanned the room. A table, bookshelves, chairs, sofa, paper, books, and a ladder.

That's it. The ladder.

Joon wasn't going to like this idea of mine, but it was the best one. And it would work as long as I did it correctly.

"I figured it out. But before you say no, just remember this is the only way."

"What is your genius idea?"

I pointed to the ladder leaning against the bookshelves. "I'm going to make that bigger."

He stared at me and cocked his head. "I don't know, Lia. Remember the last time you did that spell?"

"Yes! And it worked!" I jumped up excitedly.

"Kind of," he said.

"Well, something did get bigger," I said. "So it worked."

I just needed to focus and block everything out. I zeroed in on the ladder and chanted, "Keojigeora."

The wood crackled and a rung appeared.

Joon jumped up and ran to the ladder. "You did it!"

I clasped my fingers together and stretched my arms. "Okay, here I go."

Every time I chanted, a new rung appeared. I repeated it until the ladder almost touched the floating books.

Before I could stop him, Joon raced up the ladder. "Which book should I get first?"

"Oh, I know. We should get more info on the dragon."

He looked at the covers of the books in front of him. "Not here. You need to push the ladder over there."

Just looking at him high up there made me dizzy. I leaned my body against the ladder, but nothing happened. It was too tall and heavy.

Only one thing to do. I stepped back and pictured the ladder moving a little to the left. "Umjigyeora."

Joon yelped as the ladder shifted. "A little warning next time!" He picked a book up and threw it down. It landed with a thud on the floor.

I was about to grab it when Joon yelled, "Stand back."

He threw a few more books down. "Anything else?"

What else did we need? The only other thing I thought of was Gaya. "The evil diviner." I was pretty sure he knew what I was talking about.

He chuckled and threw down a few more books.

I gathered the books and dumped them on the table. Joon climbed down the ladder and jumped off the second-to-last rung.

"Show-off," I said as I handed him two books. "Here. Let's look for how to find the dragon." We sat down on the chairs with our own pile of books. The first book I had was called *The History of Silla*. I flipped through the table of contents and shrieked when I saw a chapter titled "The Dragon King."

"Did you find something?" He scooted next to me and peered over my arm.

"Shhhh. Still skimming." My eyes scanned down the page, searching for the word *dragon*. On the third page, I finally hit the jackpot.

I pointed with my finger and showed Joon the page.

He read out loud, "It says, 'According to legend, King Munmu turned himself into a dragon to protect the kingdom.'"

"So the dragon used to be a king!" How cool was that?

"It's a legend. I don't see how this helps us." He handed the book back to me.

I sighed. He was such a party pooper. This was just the beginning of our research. I read further. "And he hid the jewel because it was too powerful and dangerous for a human to have," I said excitedly.

Joon looked up from his book. "So Gaya thinks this dragon and jewel are real?"

"Yeah. Obviously." We studied monsters because we were trained to kill them. But dragons and the other guardian myths were just that. I didn't think I'd heard about any sightings of them.

I closed the book and picked up the second one. This one was skinny, twenty pages at most, and titled *The Legend of the Dragon*.

I turned the pages, hoping to find some clue on how to find the dragon, but I wasn't having much luck. The very last page had a paragraph on the mysterious jewel.

"This says the jewel makes your powers stronger and can heal, grant wishes, and even turn back time. It's very dangerous in the wrong hands, which is why it is guarded by the dragon." I closed the book ceremoniously. "Two for two. I'm awesome."

He didn't seem to be listening to me.

"I got something!" he shouted. "So it says here there's a temple called Gameunsa that King Munmu's son built in honor of him after he passed away."

"Is it still around?"

"Not really," Joon said. "Most of it's gone except for two tiny stone pagodas."

He held up his hand. "Well, here's the best part. After his dad became a dragon, apparently the son hid a bamboo flute at the temple that he played when he missed his father. This is the only bamboo flute that has the power to summon the dragon."

"If the temple's no longer there, how are we going to find this bamboo flute?"

"It's all legend anyway," he said. "But we should check it out just in case."

I nodded in agreement. It wouldn't hurt to go look around. Maybe there was actually something there. Ever since I'd gotten to Korea, there'd been a surprise around every corner. I hoped there was some truth to this legend.

Joon stood up and stretched his arms. He looked around and asked, "How do we get out of here?"

"Don't know. But before we go, let's see if there's something on Gaya." If there was anything I'd learned from my boring IMA classes, it was to know your enemy.

"Go for it," he said as he sat back down.

I picked up the book titled *History of Famous Diviners* and flipped through until I reached Gaya's chapter.

"What exactly does a diviner do?" Joon asked.

"Were you sleeping in class?"

"Ugh. Lia, hurry up." He tapped on my book.

"Diviners were supposedly these special people who could control natural elements," I said. "Back then they thought diviners could speak to the gods, so there were all these rituals they performed to bring rain."

"But they don't exist anymore."

I nodded and went back to reading from the book. "Hmmm. Interesting."

"What is?"

"This says her real name is Gayoung. The king of Gaya loved her so much that he nicknamed her Little Gaya, so that everyone would know that she was his heart and his everything."

"That's actually kind of sweet," Joon said with a smile. "But did you say king of Gaya? As in the Gaya Kingdom from the Three Kingdoms period? Isn't that from the 300s?"

I furrowed my brows, clearly annoyed that he was interrupting me. "Well, actually it says here she was active during the mid-500s."

"What? How is she even alive?"

"Who knows? Magic, I guess. Can I continue, please?" Maybe she was a vampire. Or a zombie. It was without a doubt very strong magic if it kept her alive this long.

"Go ahead."

"One night Silla's Hwarang warriors attacked the palace and assassinated the Gaya king."

"That's terrible," Joon said.

Even though I didn't do it, as a member of the Hwarang I felt bad. I skimmed the next couple lines and said, "Well, it gets worse."

"Hurry up and read it."

"She was being chased by the Hwarang, so she hid her baby. But there was a full-on battle at this point, and she couldn't locate her baby again."

He shook his head. "As evil as she is, I'm so angry for her."

I had to agree with him on this one. What was done to her was horrible. "And to top everything off, the Gaya Kingdom disappeared after that night and became a part of Silla."

Those people probably turned her evil. She must've been so heartbroken to lose so many people she loved and even her country in a single night. "If I were her, I'd be devastated and want revenge," I said.

Joon flipped through the book. "What do you think happened to her baby?"

"Who knows? But I'd do anything to get my baby back."

And then it hit me. I knew exactly why Gaya wanted the jewel.

CHAPTER 16

"What? What is it?" Joon peered into my face. "You look like you saw a ghost."

A shiver crawled up my spine and I shuddered. "Don't you get it?"

"No." He sighed and paced back and forth. "Spill it."

I clenched my fists and tried to figure out the best way to tell him. "Okay. But this is a big one."

"Oh, come on. Enough with the theatrics. Tell me already."

I took a deep breath and patted the chair next to me. "Sit."

Joon rolled his eyes and groaned as he sat down. "This better be good."

"Gaya's trying to get her baby back," I said slowly.

"Her lost baby?" He scrunched up his face.

I sighed. Why wasn't he getting it? "That's why she wants the jewel."

"I'm so confused," Joon said.

"The jewel has powers to turn back time, right?"

"Yeah."

"So she wants the jewel to turn back time and find her baby." But the second I said it, I knew there was so much more. "If you lost everything, wouldn't you want to get it all back?"

His eyes widened in fear. "I don't know. Maybe."

"That's such a lie. I know you, and you would," I argued. "I'd do anything to get my parents back. It's the same thing."

"Okay, okay. You're right."

I continued, "She's going to turn back time so she can find her baby, save the king, and protect her country."

"And recover everything and everyone she's lost," Joon added.

He paused, and then continued, "Say everything you just told me is true. Then what would happen to us?"

He was definitely not going to like my answer. I took a deep breath and said, "Well, obviously, we wouldn't be alive."

"We'd be dead?" His eyes bulged out.

"If she turns back time," I said, my voice shaking, "the present as we know it will be no more. The whole world will change to whenever she was around. Like to when she was alive during the Gaya Kingdom. So the 550s, maybe."

"Oh no. This is bad."

"It's worse than bad," I said. "She wants to rewrite history."

Joon's face paled and his voice trembled. "We'd never exist. Ever."

Now he was finally catching on. Took him long enough. "Exactly."

"We have to stop her!" He stood up and stretched out his hand. "Come on."

I grabbed his hand and got up. "We need to get out of here."

"How?" Joon said, looking around. "There aren't any doors here."

In all the excitement of seeing the flying books, I'd forgotten about the clue I'd found earlier. I reached inside my pocket and pulled out the piece of paper. "Maybe this will help." I opened the paper. "'What you wish we could build at home / Our favorite childhood book / < Pull > .'"

"So, any idea what it means?"

I walked to the bookshelves and remembered asking my parents to build me a secret passageway through the bookcase in my room for my birthday. Just like in the movies.

We'd tried pulling on the books before and nothing happened. Maybe only certain books came out. "What are you thinking?" asked Joon.

"The answer to the clue is a secret passageway through the bookshelf. And we just have to find my parents' favorite book, *The Green Frog*."

It was about a frog who didn't like to listen to his mom. Whatever she asked him to do, he'd do the opposite. One day she got really sick and told him if she died, to leave her body in the stream. She thought he would do the opposite. But the little green frog felt bad for not listening to his mom. So he did exactly what she asked and cried as she floated away. It was the worst story ever.

He chuckled. "You really think we'll find it?"

For some reason I felt very sure of my answer. After all, who knew me better than my parents? "My parents know what I love."

"Let's go for it." He ran his finger along the spines of the books.

"We should split up. You go start from the other end." He raced over to the other side of the room.

After going through several rows, I finally found the book and was about to pull it out when Joon placed his hand on my arm and stopped me.

"You know what? I should do it, just in case. I'm the invincible one, remember?" He winked and motioned for me to back up.

He pulled at the book, but it barely budged.

I smacked my head. The green frog did the opposite of what his mom asked, so that meant I needed to do the opposite of pulling.

"Push it in instead," I said.

"Okay, here goes." He pushed the book in, and an unsettling hissing noise filled the air. Before I knew it, a bolt of fire shot out from the book.

I screamed, "Duck!" and dropped to the floor. The heat from the fire warmed the top of my head.

Joon was a little slow, and the fire grazed his hand. "Ow!" His face scrunched up in pain.

I grabbed his hand. The skin on the back of his hand was burned off, and all I could see were redness and blistering. "I think I might have some Band-Aids, except they definitely aren't big enough to cover your hand." I reached inside my bag.

"It's okay." He grabbed my hand, stopping me. "I'll heal."

I'd totally forgotten about that. His one amazing super-power was to heal himself. I hugged him and tried to blow on his hand to help it to stop hurting.

He flinched and jerked his hand away. "That hurts more, and I can smell your breath."

I punched him in the arm.

"Ow!" He yelped in pain. "I'm still human, you know."

I turned around, grabbed a piece of gum from my bag, and quickly popped it into my mouth. *Hmph.* I knew I definitely did not have bad breath but wasn't willing to take any chances.

"See?" He lifted his burned hand to my face.

My eyes bulged as a new layer of skin started to cover the redness. The blisters grew smaller and disappeared. "That's amazing. Does it hurt when it heals?"

He shrugged. "Not really. I just feel a tingly, bubbly sensation."

I stood up to take a closer look at the book. It should have worked if I was going with the special book logic. I blinked and let out a frustrated sigh.

"Look." I pointed at the spine of the book. "The frog next to the title is purple. Not green."

He stared at the title. "I didn't even notice there was a picture of a frog."

"There must be decoys," I said, scanning another row for the right one.

Joon whistled and blew out some air. "Dang. Your parents are geniuses."

"Yeah. They do think of everything. Pretty paranoid, if you ask me." I heard Appa's voice in my head. *Lia, don't rush. Take your time.*

Joon mumbled to himself as he ran his finger across a row of books. "Nope. Nope. Nope."

I took a deep breath and focused on the titles in front of me. My eyes flitted across the shelves. Deep in my heart, I just knew it had to be here somewhere.

After an hour of searching, I finally found the right one. "Joon! It's here!"

I pointed at it. "See? This frog is green."

He looked closely at the spine of the book. "Yeah, this must be the right one."

I took a deep breath and with a shaky finger reached for the book. "Moment of truth."

Joon stopped me. "I'll do it."

At least if this blew up, he could heal himself again.

I moved aside and coached him. "Bend your knees and get ready to duck as soon as you push it."

He nodded and pushed it. A loud creaking sound echoed through the room. I jumped back and huddled next to Joon. The bottom five shelves started to turn.

"This is so cool!" Joon whispered in my ear.

"It so is." I pressed my hands together and touched them against my lips.

In no time at all, the bookshelves swiveled around and opened like a door. A musty smell wafted up my nose, probably because the passageway hadn't been opened in forever. But the stranger thing was the music.

I cupped my hand to my ear. Faint but distinct sounds came from behind the bookshelves. "Do you hear that?"

"I do. What is that?"

I moved closer to the bookshelves and peered inside.

A dark tunnel with tiled floors and walls made of stones stretched out before me. As I stepped into the tunnel, all the torches lit up with a sizzle. I gasped and stared at the ground. It looked like the same tiles that we had in our backyard at home. Maybe it was a popular tile.

Joon stood next to me. "I think I know this song."

I nodded. Now that we were inside the tunnel, the

song was softly playing through invisible speakers. My eyes welled up. "Appa and I used to dance to this song every night after dinner."

"No way." Joon looked up at the ceiling. "I have no idea where the music is coming from." He walked into the tunnel and touched the walls.

Whooshing sounds broke the silence as arrows flew across the tunnel. Joon ducked out of the way but not before an arrow grazed his arm.

"What the . . ." Joon stood up and wiped off the blood from his arm.

Even though he could heal himself, it sucked to see him getting hurt so many times because of me.

I started to move toward him when he yelled, "Don't move." He stood up and planted his feet firmly on the ground. "This place is booby-trapped."

"Of course it is." I didn't mean to sound snarky, but my parents had really outdone themselves with this one. I'd just about had it with all their unnecessary obstacles.

"You're lucky it's so hard for me to die, or you would've gotten me killed by now." He chuckled.

Really? This was not the time to be joking. I already felt guilty about everything. "Yeah. Good thing." I couldn't think of any witty comebacks.

"Well, just like before, this is all you. Your puzzle to solve." He pretended to take his hat off and bowed.

I closed my eyes and listened to the song. Before I knew it, I was singing along. Umma and Appa had their wedding song, and they'd dance to it every night after dinner. I remembered I got so jealous once that I made myself cry. Appa picked me up and said that we could have our special song too. Ever since that day, this had been our song.

I stood up and bopped to the music. I knew how to get through this tunnel.

"Earth to Lia!" Joon waved with his hands. "Snap out of it!"

I opened my eyes and smiled. "Don't worry. I got this." The song was on repeat, so I just needed to wait until it got back to the beginning again. "Follow me exactly!"

When the intro began, I counted loudly, "One, two, three." I took two steps forward, one step to the right, and another step to the left. This landed me right behind Joon.

"Copy what I'm doing," I yelled. I took two steps forward, one step to the right, one step back, two steps forward, and two steps to the left. "Stay in place here and sway, sway, sway." I looked back to see him following along. "Almost there."

I took one step back, two steps forward, one step to the right, two steps forward, and swayed three times. Then, for the finale, I jumped in the air and landed on the tile in front of me.

Joon jumped and landed right next to me. "That was insane."

I laughed. "You had some good moves."

He gave a thumbs-up and patted himself on the back. "How did you remember all that?"

My face turned red. "Oh, I could do that in my sleep."

"I'm just glad we got out of that alive." He walked ahead and turned the corner.

A wooden elevator opened as soon as we walked near it.

"I guess this is our ride," I said.

We linked arms and walked inside. The doors creaked shut, but there were no buttons of any kind on the walls.

With a jolt, the elevator moved upward. It stopped as abruptly as it had started, and the doors creaked open.

CHAPTER 17

I don't know what I'd been expecting to see on the other side of the door, but what greeted us was nothing but wooden walls all around us. A complete dead end. The elevator door slammed shut behind us.

We were trapped in a tight tunnel, with nowhere to go but up. The space was so small that we couldn't even stand shoulder to shoulder.

I found it harder to breathe and gagged.

"Are you okay?" Joon stood right behind me and patted my back.

"Yeah. Just a little claustrophobic," I mumbled.

He pounded against the elevator door, but nothing

happened. As soon as he stopped, I felt a gush of air blowing from the ground. My hair flew up, and I could feel the skin on my cheeks lifting up. I couldn't even open my mouth to scream. Joon pressed his arms against both sides of the tunnel. I followed his lead, but my arms trembled from the sheer force of the air.

Whatever was supposed to happen had to be better than breaking both my arms. I squeezed my eyes shut and let go of the walls. Joon flashed me an are-you-out-of-your-mind look.

The air grew stronger, and I zipped up though a wooden tunnel. I pressed my arms against my sides. *Please, please, please let us make it through this in one piece.*

With a thud, I landed on something hard and bumpy. A couple seconds later, Joon crashed next to me. I smiled as the sun warmed my face, and I took a deep breath of fresh air. But when I opened my eyes, all I saw were branches and leaves. I screamed and rocked backward. Joon gripped my arm and pulled me forward.

We stared at each other and started laughing. *Daebak.* I was happy to be alive, and it was crazy that we'd just shot up through the inside of a tree and were now perched on a branch.

Joon was already climbing down. "It's not too bad. Put your foot over there."

I turned around and looked for a branch below me. Then I found another one. This was the lowest branch. I held on to it with both my hands and swung my legs off from it.

"Just let go!" he yelled.

One, two, three.

I took a deep breath before pushing myself off. I tumbled onto the ground and groaned in pain.

Joon stuck out his hand. He couldn't stop grinning. "Unbelievable!"

I dusted off my pants and looked up at the tree, which looked so normal. Who could've guessed there was some secret elevator inside? "Yeah. That was." There were trees everywhere, and not a single person in sight. It looked like we were near the bottom of a hill.

"Where are we, anyway?" Joon asked.

I studied my map and shook my head. "No idea."

A familiar chirping sound filled my ears. A swallow flew toward us and circled above our heads. I pointed at the bird. "She found us! It's Halmoni!"

Uh-oh. I was going to have some explaining to do. I hoped she wasn't too mad.

We jumped up and waved. The bird circled above our heads and flew over the hill.

"Let's follow her." I trudged up the hill. The ground was a little muddy but not too slippery.

At the top of the hill there was a clearing with a stunning view of the ocean. And nothing around except two pagodas with three tiers each.

Halmoni perched on top of a large sign with some writing on it.

Without saying a single word, we sprinted toward it.

"Got here first!" Joon yelled.

I stood next to him and read the sign. "It says this was Gameunsa Temple, although there's not much left of it."

Halmoni flew down, and blue sparks encircled her as she transformed. I rushed over to hug her. It was so good to see her all better again. "I'm sorry I didn't listen to you. I just wanted to find the jewel for my parents."

"My Lia, I know. And you did so well. I'm so proud of you." She kissed my cheek and then stretched out her arms to Joon. "You did a great job watching out for her."

He blushed and said, "I didn't do much. We did it together."

"Are you all better now, Halmoni?" I checked her arms and legs for any bleeding.

"Yes. Magic wounds can heal fast if treated with the right medicine. And you, my dear, took me to the doctor right away."

I hugged her close and rested my head against her shoulder. "I'm so glad you're okay." I couldn't wait to tell her about what we had done today. "Did you know about the magic library? And I can do magic really well now!"

She chuckled and squeezed my cheeks. "You are my granddaughter after all. And yes, the library's been in our family forever. So that's where your parents sent you?"

I nodded. "It was amazing. We found out that the bamboo flute to summon the dragon is here."

Joon looked at the remains of the temple. "So where is it?"

Halmoni shrugged. "I never had to find it myself, so I don't know."

"Well, that's what it said in the book we found in the library." I placed my hands on my hips and stared at the two pagodas, which were a little taller than me. "It's probably hidden with some magic."

"Obviously. Safe to say magic seems to be the theme for the day." Joon was already checking the bottom of a pagoda.

"You're hilarious," I huffed, and walked toward the other pagoda with Halmoni.

He was so impatient. I bet he didn't even check it that well. I made a mental note to myself to recheck the other pagoda after this.

The pagoda was gray and felt bumpier than I expected under my fingers. I tiptoed and ran my hand over the top layer. Tilting my head, I looked underneath but didn't find anything interesting. I ran my hand over the second tier and again found nothing unusual.

There was only one tier left to go. I quickly ran my hands over the top and then crouched down to peek underneath. To my surprise, there was an engraving. "There's something here!"

Halmoni held my bag as I lay down on the ground and reached up to touch the engraving.

"What did you find?" Joon was already bending down next to me to catch a glimpse of it.

"Don't know yet." I traced the symbol with my fingers. A shiver went up my spine. I scooted out from under the pagoda and reached for my bag.

"Let me see." Joon laid down on the ground and studied the marking.

"Hold on." I searched around inside my bag until my hand closed on the flat circular shape of the coin I'd found in my house.

"Joon, excuse me."

He inched over a little to the left and made space for me.

I pulled out the red coin and lay down under the pagoda again. When I held it up to the engraving, I couldn't believe my eyes. "It's the same symbol!" I opened my palm and showed Joon. Then I stood up and gave the coin to Halmoni.

Halmoni flipped the coin back and forth. "Where did you get this?"

"That's what Umma and Appa left for me," I said. "And it transported us to Seoul."

Halmoni beamed and gave it back to me. "My Mira is so clever. Making this old thing multifunctional."

This old thing? What did she mean by that? "You've seen this before?"

"Of course," she said. "This used to be mine, and my grandmother's before that. It's been in our family for generations."

"So how do we use it?" I pointed at the squiggly symbol on the coin. "Do you know what this means?"

Halmoni rubbed her thumb over it. "It's the ancient symbol of the dragon." She handed the coin back to me. "But no one's ever had to use it. I always thought the story about the temple and the coin was just a legend."

Joon and I huddled around her. "What's the story, Halmoni?"

She looked up and thought for a minute. "As you know, King Munmu's son created this temple for his father, who became the Dragon King and keeper of the jewel."

I nodded. "Yes, we read that in the books back in the library."

"He hid the bamboo flute in the temple, but before he locked it up . . ." She pointed to the coin and continued, "He created a magic key."

I couldn't help grinning. We were so close to finding the jewel and saving my parents now. "So how do we unlock it?"

"The legend says that when the twin symbols meet, the bamboo flute shall greet."

"Huh? What does that mean?" asked Joon.

Another riddle. Good thing I was a master at figuring them out, thanks to years of deciphering treasure hunt clues. "Twin symbols" must mean the same ones. And "meet" must mean that they needed to be in the same place or on top of each other. We were standing near the pagoda with the coin and nothing happened, so it must mean to put the two symbols together.

I jumped up and down. "I got it!"

I laid down and pressed the coin onto the engraving on the pagoda.

The coin started whistling and glowing in my hands, and grew to twice its size. I yelped and dropped it.

As soon as I dropped the coin, it went back to its normal size.

Halmoni picked it up and nudged me aside. "I'll hold it down. You two, go look for the bamboo flute."

I nodded and hugged her.

She knelt down and pressed the coin against the underside of the pagoda.

A low rumbling sound came from under our feet. A cracking sound filled the air as the ground began to split open.

"Run!" Joon grabbed my hand, and we ran to the sign and hid behind it.

The ground all around us was splitting and forming trenches. But it didn't seem random. Like if there were an earthquake, the cracks on the ground wouldn't form a pattern of any kind. But here, there were some grooves that were perpendicular, a few circular shapes, while others were straight lines.

"What is that?" Joon shouted.

"Don't know!" It was hard to concentrate with the ground moving beneath us.

After what seemed like forever, everything grew silent. We peeked out from behind the sign and gasped at the sight before us. The deep grooves in the ground weren't random but formed the ancient symbol of the dragon.

"Oh my gosh. That's crazy." I knelt down and touched one of the trenches with my hands.

The bottom half of the symbol, which looked like a curved tail, extended all the way to the edge of a cliff facing the ocean.

Water gushed from the pagodas and filled the symbol.

I pointed to something brown floating in the trenches. "Wait! Wait! Look at that!"

It was cylindrical, with three holes and a mouthpiece. The bamboo flute.

Joon raced over to grab it but missed. "It's headed your way! Catch it!"

I saw the flute floating toward me. I wanted to say water was not my thing, but that didn't seem important right now. All I needed to do was dip my hand in and pick it out. This was shallow water. Just like washing my hands. No big deal.

I took a deep breath and grabbed the flute.

My hands shook as I sat down on the grass.

Halmoni and Joon crouched next to me.

"Play it." Halmoni put her arm around my shoulders. "This is all you."

I took a deep breath and blew into the flute, but nothing happened. That was strange. I cocked my head and felt my face turn red. After taking in another big gulp of air, I blew into the flute. Nothing.

I squinted my eye and peered inside the flute. Maybe there was something jammed inside that was keeping the sound from coming out.

"Maybe that's not the right flute," said Joon.

"No. This is the right one." I showed Joon the dragon engraving on the back of it.

Why wasn't it working? I held the flute up to my lips and puffed out my cheeks.

Joon pointed at black smoke billowing from the front pocket of my bookbag. "Watch out!"

I shrieked, and he kicked my bag with his foot. The smoke seeped out of my bag and swirled around in front of me.

I clutched Halmoni's hand. This was a trap, and we'd walked right into it. "Run!" The sky was littered with streaks of black smoke, all headed straight for us. I didn't even have to look to know what was going to happen next. I shuddered at the familiarity of it all. In a matter of seconds, the smoke started to take shape, and I could make out the beginnings of arms and legs.

We ran to hide behind one of the pagodas.

Halmoni rolled up her sleeves. "You guys run and get that flute away from here."

There was no way I would leave her again. I was stronger now too. "We stay together."

"I'll distract them. You two should go." Joon took the flute from me and jammed it into his pocket before breaking into a sprint across the field.

Why were they not getting it? We were stronger together. That was our only chance of defeating these shadows.

The shadows turned and flew after him. My lips trembled as the shadows caught up. I wanted to shout and warn Joon, but nothing came out of my mouth.

Joon ducked underneath the shadows' outstretched arms and scampered away. This time the shadows turned back into smoke and encircled him.

"Run, Lia!" The smoke wrapped around his entire body.

Only cowards ran. I swiveled around and bolted toward him. Joon groaned as the shadows squeezed tighter.

Halmoni waved her arms in the air and screeched. A flock of birds flew over our heads. She pointed at the shadows holding Joon, and the birds immediately attacked. But the shadows flung one bird at a time off with such force that the birds lay still on the ground.

Joon looked at me and held the flute out as far as he could reach. I lunged for it, but the shadows' grip on him tightened, hiding the flute.

I searched for Halmoni and saw blue sparks fly out of the corner of my eye as she transformed back into a swallow.

"No!" What was she doing? The birds were no match for the shadow. It would destroy her in seconds.

I army-crawled toward Joon, hoping to avoid detection. "Drop it now!"

Halmoni flew above the shadows, distracting them.

Joon dropped the flute, and it fell near his feet. I snatched it and stuffed it into my pocket.

He mouthed, "Go," and flicked his wrist.

I shook my head and stood up. Leaving him behind wasn't an option.

I dug my feet into the ground and yanked on the shadows. I grunted as I pulled with all my might. A shadowy arm reached out and slipped the flute out of my pocket. I reached up and grabbed the flute. The shadow lifted me up into the air as I clung on. Halmoni flew into the air and attacked the shadows by biting them. Instead of flinching, one of them grabbed her and stuffed her in its mouth.

I screamed and cried as I watched Halmoni disappear. Without showing any sign of relenting, the shadow holding the flute swung me from side to side. I gagged from the dizziness but held on to the flute with every ounce of strength I could muster. After a couple minutes, my fingers started to slip. I cried out and landed with a thump on the ground. The flute flew through the air and crashed against the stone pagoda.

I stood up, ready to fight, but the shadows disappeared, taking Joon and Halmoni with them.

Tears trickled down my face. I picked up the pieces of the broken flute and slumped down against a mini pagoda. In a matter of days, I'd managed to lose my parents and hurt my grandma, and failed to save my friend.

I threw the flute pieces on the ground. This had all been for nothing. I punched the grass with my fists as my heart tightened inside my chest.

I wrapped my arms around my legs and rested my head on my knees. If only I'd checked the front pocket of my bookbag, I would've discovered the stowaway shadow. Back at the train station, I felt a presence following me, but I didn't see anything. I had checked everywhere except for that one front pocket because I never put anything in there. Gut instincts were one of an agent's most prized asset, and I should've known better than to dismiss the uneasiness I felt. Such an amateur and reckless move on my part, which put all of us in danger.

This was all my fault.

CHAPTER 18

Defeated, I crumpled onto the grass and stared out at the ocean with tears in my eyes. I felt numb and unable to move. Everything had happened so fast. One minute we were all together, and the next I was alone. I'm not sure what my parents had been hoping to teach me with the treasure hunt, but all I know was that I'd failed big time.

My heart wrenched at the thought of continuing by myself.

My last hope had been to use the flute to summon the dragon. Now that was gone too. Having the fate of my parents and the world on my shoulders came crashing down.

Joon had helped me keep going, and no matter how bad the situation, I'd believed there was a way. I just couldn't see it anymore.

The only friend I'd ever known was gone. We were supposed to do this together. My arms drooped, and I lay down on the grass. Nothing mattered anymore.

The grass rustled against my fingers. I turned my head to see the four broken pieces of the flute begin to glow and levitate. Magic.

This was definitely the right flute. I sat up and wiped my face. Who knew why it was doing this now? But maybe, just maybe, I still had a chance to find the jewel and save everyone and the world.

I bolted up and ran to pick the pieces up. But before I could, the floating pieces, like magnets, clicked onto each other. I jumped around, hoping to grab the repaired flute, but it flew just beyond my reach.

The flute, now transformed into a golden hue, floated higher into the sky and zipped toward the ocean. I stared with my mouth hanging open.

The water glistened under the sun, and the waves lapped gently against the rocks. In the middle of the ocean, the waves began to swirl like a whirlpool. The hole in the ocean glowed as the flute drew closer. It froze in midair above the hole and played a soothing and sad tune that I had never heard before.

With a gust of wind and a flash of light, a woman dressed in a black hanbok with silver floral decorations materialized and gracefully landed on the grass in front of me. Her hair was braided and wrapped in an intricate bun on top of her head. I recognized her face immediately. It was hard to ignore how strikingly beautiful she was. Almost regal.

"Gaya," I muttered under my breath.

"Lia," she said as she glared at me. "I see you've found the flute."

All the fear left my body and I glared at her. "You evil person. Give me back my family and my friend."

She smirked and flicked open both her hands. A holographic image of my parents, Halmoni, and Joon appeared before my eyes. They stood with their hands and feet tied and mouths gagged.

I knew they weren't really there, but I reached out anyway to touch Umma. My hand went right through her.

Gaya said, "You didn't think I would actually bring them here, now, did you?"

"Guess not." Two could play this game. Didn't know if it'd work or not, but I had to try. I closed my eyes and pictured my family and Joon next to me and chanted silently, *Idong. Move my family here.* I'd just transport them and beat her at her game. Instead of feeling the little spark in my body when a spell worked, I felt nothing.

Gaya sneered and cupped my face with her hands. "Silly girl. Did you really think you could beat me by using your spellmaker powers?" She pointed to the holographic images. "Spellmakers aren't all-powerful. You can't just transport people."

My heart sank, but I refused to give up. "If you want the jewel, then I want to see them in real life."

"Fair point. You need motivation. I get it." She raised one arm in the air and closed her hand one finger at a time. In a matter of seconds, a gagged Joon materialized in front of her. She looked startled and winced as she grabbed him. Whatever pain it looked like she was feeling had been momentary. She composed herself, and the cold expression I'd come to know returned. With a snap of her fingers, a knife appeared, and she placed it aggressively against Joon's throat. She glowered at me and taunted, "I dare you to try."

I swallowed hard and held back a whole bunch of ugly words. Joon's life was hanging by a thread, and I needed to keep my cool and make sure he survived this. I wanted to run to him and hug him. But I knew she wouldn't allow it. "Joon. Are you okay?"

Despite having a knife to his neck, he nodded ever so slightly. He grunted and rubbed his chest.

"Now bring me the jewel, and I'll give them all back to you," she said between labored breaths.

Joon, Halmoni, and my parents all shook their heads. I knew what they were trying to tell me. Destroying the jewel was more important than their lives. Which was so not true. I would figure something out, but there was no way I was going to let them die.

Gaya hunched over and pursed her lips. She looked over at my parents and wagged her finger at them. "Naughty, naughty." She stared at me and said, "If you don't bring me the jewel, I can promise you they will die the worst deaths possible."

She closed her hand, one finger at a time, and Joon and the image of my family disappeared.

"Bring them back!"

"Certainly." A holographic image of Joon and my family reappeared before me. But this time attached to everyone's right leg was a massive rock.

I panicked. There was no way I could save them if they

were sinking in the ocean. "Even if I wanted to, I don't even know where it is."

She chuckled. "Silly girl." She pointed to the flute as it glowed and hovered in the air over the middle of the ocean. "That's the entrance."

All the muscles in my body tightened as I stared out at the blue water and crashing waves. Uncontrollable fear pounded over me, and I stood there, frozen. There was no way I could do this.

"I'm bored. Maybe you need more motivation." The rope tying the rock around Appa's leg loosened. Gaya twirled her finger, and watery arms wrapped around Appa's body and lifted him up into the air.

I shrieked as I watched the image of Appa spinning lifelessly like a doll.

I managed to shout in between sobs, "Stop! Stop!"

Gaya cackled and continued to twirl her finger, which made the watery arms holding Appa spin faster.

I couldn't watch this anymore. "Stop! Please! I'll do what you want." I dropped to my knees and rubbed my hands together and pleaded. I knew begging wasn't the way to win anything, but I couldn't watch her hurt him anymore. If it meant I had to go into the water, then that was what I was going to do.

Gaya lowered her hand, and I watched the holographic image of Appa collapse onto the ground. Umma knelt down next to him and dropped onto his chest. Her body heaved up and down as she cried.

"Are you ready now?"

I nodded and stood up.

"That's my good girl." She nudged me forward, closer to the water.

Before I went, I needed to make sure of something to find closure. "It was you all those years ago, wasn't it?"

"I'm offended you're just remembering me now. I've been thinking about you and tracking you all these years. My precious little key."

My stomach churned at the thought of being her precious anything. "My family and friend for the jewel."

"Of course." She spoke with such hatred in her eyes. "Now, go on."

As I forced myself to walk to the edge of the cliff, Umma screamed and shook her head violently. I gazed back at her and put on my bravest smile—an I-know-what-I'm-doing smile. How much I loved them was all she needed to understand.

"I'll be okay, Umma. Don't worry." I lifted my hand in a hesitant wave and then gave her a thumbs-up sign. It broke my heart to see Umma so worried for me. I knew she'd do anything to keep me safe and stop me from jumping into that water. But now it was my turn.

Tears blurred my vision, but I forced myself to keep walking and not look back. Seeing me cry would crush my parents. I wanted them to remember me in this moment as the brave one.

I stopped at the edge of the cliff and looked out at the water. Panic crawled up my arms, threatening to overwhelm me with fear. Memories of happier times back home in California, before all of this, flooded my mind. My heart warmed, and I felt renewed strength bubble up inside of me. This was for them.

Even though the water still terrified me, a wave of peace swept over me in knowing that whatever happened next, at least I would have bought my family and Joon a bit of time to figure out how to escape. I'd take that chance any day over watching everyone I loved drown right in front of my eyes.

I held my nose and readied myself. All I had to do was jump . . . and then somehow manage to get to that swirling hole in the middle of the ocean. No big deal.

Now or never. I squeezed my eyes shut and leaped off the cliff.

The wind rushed against my face, and for a moment I floated down through the air, light as a feather.

Then I crashed into the unforgiving ice-cold water. I couldn't move at all and felt myself sinking. Thrashing my arms didn't do much except drain my energy. I opened my eyes and kicked my legs as fast as I could.

A warmness in my chest took me by surprise. I looked down and gasped. My heart was glowing. It was yellowish and shining, just like the flute. I massaged my chest, hoping that it would just disappear. But I didn't have much strength left. Maybe this was the end for me. I couldn't think of a worse way to go than by the thing I feared the most.

My head popped above the water, and I gasped for air. The flute floated ahead of me, showing me the way like a beacon. I couldn't stay afloat, and I sunk down. Maybe I was delirious, but I could've sworn I heard the flute playing. But that wasn't possible. Not in the water. My heart glowed even brighter, and a force pulled me through the water.

My eyes half closing, I turned my head to see if there was anyone or anything there. Nothing at all. No matter how hard I tried, my eyes kept drooping. I pictured my family and Joon depending on me, believing in me. I couldn't let them down.

Using my last bits of energy, I kicked. My lungs burned from holding my breath for so long. As I propelled myself into the whirlpool, I saw a golden road at the bottom. Was that the ocean floor? Why would there be a road at the bottom of the ocean?

I must be delirious from the lack of air.

As if some force was pulling me in, my chest lurched forward and I sank faster into the hole. My ears popped and I couldn't bear it anymore. I gave one last kick, and my legs went limp.

I collapsed onto something dry and soft. Like a warm, sandy beach.

CHAPTER 19

People whispered around me in a language that sounded somewhat like Korean. Water trickled down my cheeks from something cold pressed against my forehead. Another person whacked my back like their life depended on it.

My head throbbed, and I gulped in air but cringed as it burned through my chest. Maybe I'd swallowed too much water, but I couldn't find my voice. I cleared my throat but only ended up coughing. My body tightened as water spilled from my mouth.

I raised my arms to rub my eyes but couldn't move them. When I finally managed to open my eyes, I found myself sitting in a chair with something cool and green wrapped around me. Was that seaweed? I wiggled and tried to move, but the seaweed didn't budge.

A man with glasses peered down at me. I shrieked, but this only made the man inch his face closer to mine and poke my cheek. I flinched and tried to kick.

The man with the glasses backed away and in a low voice said, "She's awake, Your Majesty."

Your Majesty? Where was I?

Not only did I have a hard time keeping my eyes open, but everything also still looked blurry. Large golden curtains lined both sides of a red-carpeted path. Where the curtains ended, a couple steps led to a wooden throne with gold decorations. On the wall behind the throne was a large red circle with an animal drawn inside. I couldn't quite make out what it was from here. Not quite a snake. Maybe an eel or something else with a long body.

The whispering stopped and a hush fell across the room. People dressed in long purple robes stepped out from behind the curtains, lowered their heads, and knelt. Air blew against my cheeks, and I shivered in my still-wet clothes. A yellow dragon with antler-like horns, a long beard, and a snakelike body with scales flew through the air and across the room. It stopped in front of me. My lips quivered and all the hairs on my arm stood up as I stared into its giant bulging eyes. I wanted to look away, but its eyes were mesmerizing and sucked me in.

This must be the dragon who had the jewel. My heart leaped. That meant I'd made it. I shuddered at the thought of facing a fire-breathing dragon that liked to munch on humans, like in all the movies I'd seen. Thank goodness this was not a Western dragon but a Korean one known to be benevolent. I pursed my lips together and hoped I was right.

Golden sparks flew in the air and encircled the dragon. They swirled around him like a school of fish. Enchanted by the magic unfolding right in front of me, I waited nervously, hoping this was a good thing. Within seconds, the dragon transformed into a man with a gold crown and wearing a robe with black and gold decorations.

"Welcome, Hwarang." His voice was low but warm and inviting.

Well, at least he didn't *sound* scary.

I didn't know what to do. He stared at me, probably waiting for me to say something, which I guess was my only option. I mean, I could talk and eventually get killed, or not talk and still get killed. If I was going to die anyway, I'd rather know what was going on first. But then again, if he was going to hurt me, he would've done that already.

I inhaled deeply and decided to go for it. "Are you the dragon? How do you know who I am? And where am I?" The man with glasses frowned at me, and I quickly added, "Your Majesty."

Low whispers filled the room. A man in a blue robe standing a few feet away from me gasped and poked his friend. "Who does she think she is?"

My shoulders drooped and I lowered my head. All the blood in my body must've rushed to my face, because it was burning hot. I wanted to kick myself for asking so many questions.

When the man with the crown spoke, silence fell across the room. "Excuse them. We haven't had a visitor in centuries." He flicked his hand, and the seaweed fell off my body. "I am the Dragon King. In a past life, I was known as King Munmu." He turned to walk to the throne.

Was I supposed to follow him? I looked around for hints but was met with only blank stares. This was not a very friendly bunch.

A lady in a long blue robe with her hair tied in a bun whispered, "Follow him. And stop before the steps."

I mouthed, "Thank you," and speed-walked behind him. There was one decent person here after all.

The man with glasses scurried over to adjust the king's robe. I clasped my hands in front of me and mustered up all my strength to stand tall and look up at him.

He walked across the red carpet and up the steps, and sat down on the throne. Two golden dragons served as armrests on the chair. Everyone on either side of the carpet stood up and turned to face him.

"Wow. So you're King Munmu from the legends." This was incredible. The legends were true: when he died, he had actually turned into a dragon, the Protector of the East Sea.

"It's an honor, Your Majesty," I said, and bowed deeply.

"Tell me, Hwarang, how did you get to the Undersea Kingdom of the Immortals?" His eyebrows furrowed as he looked into my eyes.

Everyone turned to stare at me.

The weight of their eyes pinned me in place, but I tried to keep my voice from shaking when I answered. "I found the flute and tried to play it. But it broke and then pieced itself together, which was strange."

"That's because it's a magic flute that makes a sound that humans can't hear. If broken, it will always piece itself back together."

So that was what happened. It made a little more sense now.

"But how did you get here?" His eyes narrowed and he crossed his arms.

I hesitated. I didn't want to say the wrong thing and get in trouble. But surely he must know that his son had created the magical flute. I wrung my hands. "The flute opened a hole in the ocean, and I jumped into the water."

"I see." He rubbed his long white beard. "But why?"

I took a deep breath and swallowed back a lump in my throat. "Gaya. This evil diviner. She was going to kill my family and my friend if I didn't get the jewel for her."

Did he know her? I wasn't an expert on dragons, but weren't they supposed to wise? At least, the Korean ones. Maybe he did know everything that was going on and this was just a big test. I couldn't tell. This king had the best poker face.

He leaned back in his throne but said nothing, so I continued. "I can't swim, but it was the only way to save them. I had to at least try."

"Go on." He nodded, and his eyes softened.

I paused before finishing my story. Once he got the truth out of me, then what? I wasn't so sure I wanted to tell him everything, but it didn't seem like I had much choice at this point. "All I remember is that my heart started glowing just like the flute. And a force pulled me inside the whirlpool to the golden road."

The other people in the hall gasped and whispered among themselves. I couldn't hear everything, but there were definitely a few *unbelievable*s and *impossible*s floating around.

"Silence." The king patted his hands on the dragon armrests and a loud clang echoed through the room. "I asked you how you got here because only a Hwarang can find and play the flute."

Whew. That was a relief to hear.

"But only a Hwarang pure of heart can enter the Undersea Kingdom of Immortals."

I nodded as fast as I could. "I just want to save my family and my friend, Your Majesty."

"Come closer, Hwarang. I must still check."

If he believed I was a Hwarang with good intentions, he wouldn't harm me, right? But just in case, I braced myself to use magic if it came to that. Though I wasn't sure if my newbie magic would work against an actual dragon. Clenching my fists behind my back, I took a couple steps until I stood at the bottom of the stairs to the throne.

"I heard your words, but I must check the truth." He lifted his arms in the air and drew a symbol with his right hand.

Without warning, memories of my family and Joon

floated through my mind, and I smiled, though my heart ached and longed for them. The more images I saw, the more my chest throbbed and tears streamed down my face.

A single tear dropped down the Dragon King's face, and he lowered his hands. "You are true to your words and pure of heart. Without knowing whether you would get here, you sacrificed yourself to save your loved ones. For someone so young, you are brave and powerful beyond your years."

Waves of emotions crashed over me, and all I could do was kneel. "Thank you, Your Majesty. Please help me save them."

"Stand, brave Hwarang."

I pulled myself up and lifted my head.

"Only a chosen descendant of Nammo who is of age can find the jewel. Is that you?" He stroked his beard and peered into my eyes.

Chosen descendant? What if that wasn't me? I swallowed hard and answered, "Yes. I am Nammo's descendant." That much I knew for sure. Then I added, "But I don't know about the rest."

He raised his eyebrows and waved over the man in glasses, who had been standing close to the throne. Leaning back, he said, "Bring me the Book of Hwarang."

The man in the glasses bowed his head and scooted back behind a folding screen painted with mountains. Keys clanked, and a door squeaked open.

Well, this was going to be an awkward long wait. I stared at my fingers and pretended to be very interested in examining the lines on my palm. Making small talk with a king was definitely not my strong suit.

"May I ask you something, Your Majesty?"

He nodded. "What is it, young Hwarang?"

I took a deep breath and asked, "Why is Nammo the owner of the jewel?" Halmoni had never mentioned this part.

"Nammo was of royal descent. She was a princess. This jewel belongs to royal blood. Only a royal-blooded Hwarang can find and protect it."

The man with the glasses rushed out from behind the screen. Hanging his head low, he held out a discolored leather-bound book to the king.

"You may go," he said to the man with glasses. The Dragon King flipped to the last page. "What is your name?"

I cleared my throat. "My name is Park Lia."

He ran his finger down the page. "Your parents' names?"

"Chung Mira and Park Minwoo."

He closed the book and looked me up and down. "Well. You, my brave Hwarang, are indeed Nammo's last descendant."

I breathed a sigh of relief and straightened my shoulders. "Will you help me, then? I don't know where the jewel is or even what it looks like."

He cocked his head. "Let me ask you this first. What are you going to do with the jewel?"

"Gaya wants it in exchange for my parents. She wants to turn back time. Which can't happen." He nodded, as if urging me to continue.

"So what will you do? Will you take the power for yourself?" He raised his eyebrow.

I shook my head firmly. "No, Your Majesty. I want to save my family and Joon, and destroy the jewel." I hoped I sounded like I knew what I was doing when I really had no clue how to destroy it. How do you even destroy a magical jewel?

"You are the true owner of the jewel; I am just the keeper. So you may do with it as you wish."

I bowed and said, "Thank you, Your Majesty."

"But it is up to you to find and destroy it."

"How do I destroy it?"

He stroked his beard. "When good and evil collide, the jewel will be activated for destruction and change colors. Then you must create a spell to destroy it."

"Thank you." Maybe my parents or Halmoni knew the exact spell. I still needed to figure out a way to save them first.

"The jewel will test you, but a true owner will be able to find it." He leaned forward and instructed, "Once you find it, you must place the jewel in between the dragons to activate it."

That didn't make sense. But maybe once I got there, I'd know what he meant.

CHAPTER 20

Without warning, the Dragon King stood up and walked down the steps toward me. When he reached the bottom, he put his arm around me. "But first, today you will join me as my honored guest at tonight's banquet."

I knew I should accept, but what if something happened to Joon and my family while I was down here for so long? I mustered up my courage and said, "I would be honored, Your Majesty, but I cannot abandon my family and Joon."

To my surprise, he laughed out loud, and then the

whole room erupted in laughter. "Oh, my dear Hwarang Lia. I see now why you are the one."

He patted my back and nudged me to walk next to him. "Time here passes differently than in your world."

I stared back at him in surprise. Of course it did. How silly of me to think everything was the same between our two worlds. They couldn't be more different. "So I won't be gone too long?"

He nodded. "I will show you where to go to find the jewel tomorrow morning."

I must've cringed, because he smiled and added, "In your world, that would be about thirty minutes."

We walked through a maze of hallways until he stopped in front of a sliding door made of a wooden frame and covered in hanji, a Korean handmade paper. The light inside the room made the paper glow in a soft yellow tone. A young lady in purple-and-blue robes slid open the door for me.

"Bora will help you change and escort you to the banquet," said the Dragon King.

I watched him walk away as he disappeared around the corner.

"Miss, please let me show you to your quarters."

"Thank you." I didn't know what to do, so I bowed my head slightly and walked past her as she tried to stifle a giggle.

The second I stepped inside, a huge smile broke out on my face and I squealed. This was the most gorgeous room ever. I felt like a princess. The entire room was intricately but tastefully decorated. There were dark reddish-brown wooden panels with delicate gold floral designs separating the bedroom area from a larger sitting area. Surrounding the bed were sheer gray curtains with gold detailing.

On the bed lay a pale pink hanbok with dark pink bordering around the sleeves. I ran my fingers over the delicate flower embroidery and drew my hand back in shock as the flowers began to sway as if they were blowing in the wind.

Bora opened the curtains and tied them back with a golden rope with a long tassel. She pointed to a large folding screen near the bed. "Please change over there."

I walked behind the screen and quickly changed clothes. The dress fit perfectly. When I stepped out, Bora was holding a trayful of hair ornaments, ribbons, jewelry, and a comb.

She sat me down on a chair in the sitting area with a large standing mirror and placed the tray on a table next to the chair.

"You might feel a little tugging and tingling, but don't worry. That's normal."

I nodded and watched her carefully lift the comb, which had tiny flowers on it.

Bora swooped the comb through my hair once on each side, and the pink ribbons lifted off the tray. I could feel a little bit of tugging on each side and through the mirror saw the ribbons weaving themselves through my hair. She grabbed a few silver butterfly-shaped clips from the tray and tossed them up into the air. Instinctively, I closed my eyes and hoped they didn't fall on me. When nothing happened, I slowly opened my eyes and saw the butterflies flitting about and perching on different parts of my head. Then, as she gathered my hair together and lifted it above my neck, the ribbons tied my hair in place.

When I looked in the mirror, I couldn't stop smiling. I had a large braid wrapped around my head with the ribbon woven in and out. Little butterflies were spread out here and there.

For the final touch, Bora handed me long pink-beaded earrings.

"These are so pretty, but my ears aren't pierced."

Bora placed her face near mine and winked. "Have you forgotten? Everything is magic here."

She placed the earrings near my ears, and like magnets, they stuck gently. Surprisingly, I couldn't even feel them. They were so light.

"You're ready now. Please follow me." She walked to the mirror and swiped a green emerald along the sides of the wooden frame.

Instantly, the glass of the mirror disappeared, and in its place was an entrance to what seemed like an outdoor area.

"After you, Hwarang Lia."

I stepped through the mirror frame and felt my shoes crunch as I stepped on gravel. In front of me was a long, winding path that I followed. It led to a marble staircase.

"The Dragon King will be waiting for you at the top. Have a wonderful time, Hwarang Lia." She bowed and turned around to leave.

I held up my long hanbok and walked up a flight of stairs. The Dragon King, dressed in a red robe with a black belt, appeared at the top.

He reached out for me to take his hand. "Just in time, Hwarang Lia. The hanbok looks lovely on you."

I bowed my head and said, "Thank you, Your Majesty."

We walked through a cloudlike fog, and I found myself standing on top of a stage. Below us were so many people in different-colored hanbok. All around us were different podiums just floating in the air.

"The podiums are reserved for the other gods and immortals."

Just like the monsters back in the real world, everyone here looked human. It was hard to guess which immortal or god was who.

Then he pointed to the ground below us. "They are getting ready to perform a dance."

Some had swords while others held fans. A set of short round drums lined the left while larger drums lined the right. I couldn't remember exactly what kind of dance this was. "I don't think they covered this in my classes, Your Majesty."

He chuckled. "Of course not. Very few mortals get to come up here at all."

Whew. I felt better knowing I hadn't missed something in class. It was an honor to be here, and I couldn't believe that of all the people, or mortals, as he would say, I had been picked to be the one to enjoy this celebration. I just wished that I could share this moment with my family. Joon would've been in complete awe. That would've made this moment absolutely perfect.

As soon as I sat down on a chair next to the Dragon King, a table of dishes I'd never seen before appeared in front of us. There were rainbow-colored balls on gold plates. Others looked like leafy greens, but they had purple stars on the tips. Another plate had rice-cake cookies covered with little waves of water that moved. The last bowl was full of purple-and-orange apples.

The Dragon King leaned over and whispered, "Avoid the cookies. The saltiness of the waves is really strong. You'd still be able to taste it tomorrow."

I smiled and bowed my head slightly. That was a close call: it was the first thing I'd wanted to taste because I wanted to see what chewing waves would be like. Instead, I reached for a rainbow-colored ball and took a small bite. In an instant I tasted the sweetness of a ripe strawberry, the sourness of a lemon, and the savoriness of sweet yam.

It was incredible.

I opened a napkin and placed a couple of rainbow balls inside.

"Midnight snack?" asked the Dragon King.

My face turned beet red, and I wished he hadn't noticed. "I wanted my family and Joon to taste these too. They would be so amazed."

He smiled warmly and his eyes glistened. "You can try.

But most things from this realm don't make it back. They disintegrate for our and your protection."

I was a little disappointed that I wouldn't be able to share all this delicious food with them, but it totally made sense. If people knew about the stuff here, they'd do everything in their power to find this place and take it for themselves.

The sound of drums filled the air, and everyone grew silent. Women dressed in green robes with super-long sleeves started to dance in the center of the stage on the ground. As they waved their sleeves up and down, another group of women dressed in purple robes encircled them. Yet another group of women in yellow robes formed the outer circle. A second set of drums started a different beat, and all the dancers waved their sleeves in the air at the same time, creating small lotus flowers, which burst open with gold sparkles.

The crowd cheered, and I stood up and clapped. "This is truly so magical. Thank you for letting me see this."

"There's one more event, which I think you, Hwarang Lia, will love."

I sat back down and gripped my chair tightly.

This time, a group of women dressed in blue robes and a group of men in purple robes filed in and formed a triangle. They were all holding large swords. One by one they swished their swords in front of them like waves. Then they started to dance while slashing their swords back and forth. A bolt of electricity flashed across their swords and created music—heavenly music with instruments that sounded like strings and maybe some horns. I couldn't tell. But it sounded soothing and made my eyes water.

I felt a stirring in my heart, and my head was pounding again, just like it had on the bus with Joon.

Sunnyway. Umma and Appa stood in front of our street. Without speaking a word to each other, they walked around the quaint neighborhood lined with homes.

Appa picked me up and carried me tightly in his arms. I clung to him. Umma looked at me and smiled. She lifted her arms up and drew a circle in the air and chanted, "Boho." Purple, gold, and silver fireworks burst all across the sky. As the sparks fell like the droopy leaves of a willow tree, they formed a transparent dome that encapsulated the neighborhood.

"It's done," she said. "Let's go find us a home." Umma wrapped her arm around Appa's waist, and they walked down the street.

I must've passed out, because when I opened my eyes, Bora and another woman were carrying me in a cot. I tried to get up but felt so weak.

"Don't struggle. It's okay. That music is healing and unlocks mysteries in the mind," said Bora.

So that was like a vision or a memory that my parents had tried to block, but I could remember it now. My heart hurt thinking about how much my parents had given up to protect me, and all I'd done was rebel. Tomorrow I'd find the jewel and save them all.

CHAPTER 21

Last night was beyond anything I could've imagined. My headache was gone, and my strength was back. I felt refreshed this morning and more than ready to find this jewel and get back to my family.

I walked out of the room and bowed to the Dragon King, who was waiting for me.

"I hope you slept well."

"Yes, Your Majesty."

"Good, because you will need your strength."

I followed the Dragon King to the end of the hall and through an open door.

It was a massive room with glass walls. Behind the glass, giant sea turtles swam as an octopus lurked nearby. It was hard to believe that I was in the middle of the ocean somewhere. And still alive.

"This is the royal ballroom. Come along."

Along the farthest wall there were three small doors made of glass. The doors blended in perfectly with the wall.

The Dragon King stood in front of the third door. "This is it."

"How do I get inside?" There wasn't a doorknob.

"You need this first." He stepped back from me.

Sparks flew around him, and he transformed into the golden dragon. The dragon used its claws to pick off one of its scales. Another burst of light changed him back to his human form.

I hoped my mouth wasn't hanging open. Watching the transformation was really something else. Beautiful, mysterious, enchanting, and powerful. I couldn't take my eyes off him.

"Take this." He held up the golden dragon scale.

I grabbed it with both my hands. It was the size of my palm and felt smooth and cold. "Thank you, Your Majesty."

"You need to eat this, and then it's up to you to find the jewel."

I cringed at the thought of eating a scale from his body, but instead I bowed and said, "Thank you for this, Your Majesty."

He nodded and continued. "Once you eat the scale, it will take you inside. Eat half now and the other half to get back out."

"Oh. Okay." It still didn't make sense to me. How was I supposed to eat a scale? That just sounded pretty gross. I couldn't stand bugs or snakes, never mind eating part of the skin of a dragon.

"Be careful of the jewel's enchanting powers." He handed me an hourglass. "Once you're inside, you have one hour before your air runs out."

Oh great. There was also a time limit to this task. But how hard could it be to find the jewel and come back out, right? It should be a breeze.

"Wait. Do you by chance know how to destroy the jewel?"

I had to ask.

"No. Only the owner will know that. I hope you are worthy, Hwarang Lia."

"I hope so too."

He turned around and walked away.

As soon as he left, I examined the scale in my hand.

It was surprisingly soft, like a worn-in sweater. I'd never felt a dragon's scales before, but I'd thought they would be rough and hard as armor. What did he mean by "eat the scale"? Was I supposed to chew it or just swallow it without chewing? Did it even matter? And save half for later?

I held the scale up to the light but didn't find anything marking the halfway point. Maybe I just needed to eyeball it. Not willing to take any chances, I folded the scale in half. I tugged at it, but it refused to rip. On to the next best thing. I placed my index finger across the crease and took a deep breath.

I licked the scale. It tasted a bit sweet and sour at the same time, like a mixture of salt and caramel. But just in case, I plugged my nose with one hand and closed my lip over the scale until my mouth touched my index finger.

The moment my mouth closed around it, the scale melted. It felt thick, like honey or syrup. As it trickled down my throat, my head throbbed. I put the other half in my pocket and rubbed my temples in small circles, but the pain wouldn't stop. I looked down at my feet and shrieked.

I was melting into a yellowish liquid. My legs felt light, and before I could scream, they disappeared and the puddle grew larger.

They stuck to the door, climbed up, and slipped

through a vent above. My whole body turned into liquid, and I was sucked through the vent.

As soon as I got to the other side, my hands and feet grew out of the puddle, and eventually my whole body returned back to normal. I ran my hands across my face, arms, and legs and breathed a sigh of relief. Everything was back where it was supposed to be.

I looked up at the room in front of me and covered my mouth with my hands. This couldn't be it.

Along the walls were shelves completely full of jewels, crowns, necklaces, vases, and incense burners. Anything precious I could think of was here. The treasures sparkled and glowed, lighting up the entire room. The first thing I noticed was a large gold crown, without a doubt from the Silla dynasty. It had the unique gold tree branches sticking up. Small round jade pieces adorned the band, while thin golden chains swung elegantly down. It was stunning: so impressive and delicate at the same time. Nearby sat a glass ewer with a soft green hue. There were blue lines circling the neck. On a lower shelf were bowls from the Silla dynasty. They were unique because they had a pedestal with rectangular cutouts. It was thrilling to actually see pieces like the ones I've only read about in books. Except the ones here were all in perfect condition.

Mixed in with the gold coins, red, yellow, green, purple, and white jewels were scattered around all the shelves. I couldn't resist the temptation and picked up a deep purple one. It glistened as I moved it from side to side. The jewel was heavier than I expected and about as big as a baseball. I'd raided Umma's closet and tried on her necklaces, but she didn't have any jewels close to as beautiful or as big as the ones in this room. I didn't know much about jewels, but the bigger they were, the better. I bet these were worth a fortune.

On the floor in the center of the room was a design of two golden dragons with slender bodies, like snakes in circular formation. Between the two dragons' bodies was an empty round hole. I gasped when I noticed their feet. These golden dragons had seven toes. That was pretty much unheard of. I thought there was just one example left in all of Korea. Korean dragons representing kings had four claws, while Chinese dragons representing emperors had five claws. But it totally made sense, because this treasure room was at the palace of immortals, and I'm sure they ranked way above kings.

I crouched down and ran my hand over the empty hole. So this must be what the Dragon King meant when he said that I needed to place the jewel in the hole to activate it.

Oh no.

I smacked my head and dug into my pocket. I'd gotten so caught off-guard by the sheer number of treasures in the room that I'd completely forgotten to turn over the hourglass that the Dragon King gave me. I pulled it out of my pocket and flipped it over. Well, I'd already spent about five minutes in here. How do you even read fifty-five minutes on an hourglass anyway? I'd have to start hustling once only half the sand was left.

There was no time to waste. I placed the timer on a shelf next to the golden crown. Then I sifted through the jewels. Yellow. Red. Green. White. I scooped up a handful and ran over to the center of the room. Wouldn't it be amazing if the first one I put in worked? I placed one in the hole between the dragons.

A low rumbling noise shook the room, and the jewels clinked as some tumbled onto the stone floor. I jumped up and looked around. A brick from the ceiling cracked, and pieces of it crashed onto the ground. I shrieked and leaped away. Of course this place was booby-trapped too. After everything I'd been through in the last few days, how silly of me to think this would be any easier.

I quickly removed it and jammed another jewel into the hole, and another rumble shook the room. Time was running out, and I needed to cycle through the jewels. To make things move faster, I removed a jewel with my left hand and placed a new one in the hole with my right hand. With each incorrect jewel, the ceiling crumbled a little more. I coughed and wiped the dust from my eyes.

Just in case the next batch worked, I ran and dumped as many jewels as I could onto my shirt. Then I worked methodically. The ceiling shook violently and another brick crashed onto the ground. I screamed and covered my head. Thankfully, the brick landed in the corner of the room. I looked up at the ceiling and cringed at all the cracks. It would only be a matter of time before those bricks crumbled.

It seemed hopeless trying out every jewel. There must have been a million in here, and I'd tried only ten so far.

I looked at the timer and covered my eyes with my hands. I needed to think, and fast. So putting random jewels in there clearly wasn't going to work, unless I wanted the whole place to come crumbling down. I needed to be smarter about this. I closed my eyes and tried to think of a plan. My parents must have left me a clue. I racked my brain for the image of the dragon on the jewelry box. At times like this, I really wished I had Appa's photographic memory.

There was something different about that dragon, but I just couldn't remember what it was. There was a yellow body, scales, head, eyes, and a round jewel. What was I missing?

Wait.

The jewel. That was it.

It was white.

Maybe if I used my magic, I could find the real one.

I imagined the shining white jewel and whispered, "Umjigyeora." It was worth a try. I willed the jewel to come out of its hiding place and drop into my hands. I cringed and rubbed my temples to stop my head from throbbing.

There was no giving up.

I continued to chant and held out my hands. The jewels all around the room clinked and then stopped. My head pounded, and I knelt down on the floor in pain. What was happening? It felt like a hundred needles jabbing into my brain. It was hard to breathe, but I massaged my head. The pain began to disappear.

I'd never felt this before while practicing magic. Maybe the spell was too hard for me. Or maybe that was just too easy a way to find the jewel, and whoever had designed this place made sure that wouldn't work. Whatever the reason, I needed to find another way.

The white ones were mixed in all over the place. I had an idea. I calmed my mind and imagined all the white jewels floating up into the air. With a firm voice, I commanded only the white ones to move. "Umjigyeora."

Nothing happened again.

I clenched my fists and continued to chant with a sense of authority. I was a Hwarang and a spellmaker. My words and thoughts had power and it would work. It had to.

I felt my fingertips grow warm and sparks flew in the air. My eyes widened as I stared at my fingers. It was working. Only the white jewels rose from the pile and floated up into the air. They looked like glistening stars lighting up the sky.

I sliced the air with my hands and commanded them to freeze in space. Every single one of them stopped moving. Whoa. I didn't know I could do that.

I covered my mouth and held back a giggle. It felt incredible to have control over my powers. *Here's to little victories.* I fist-pumped and went back to the task at hand.

There were about one hundred white jewels floating in the air. I wouldn't have time to put each one in the dragon's mouth. Definitely didn't want to risk the room collapsing on me, either.

My eyes fell on the timer with the sand halfway gone.

Oh no. There wasn't much time left. I forced myself to take a deep breath and calm down so I could figure out my next move.

Maybe if I felt it I'd know. At least according to the Dragon King, I was the owner. And if I was somehow tied to the jewel, it should recognize me. I ran my hands across the jewels frozen in the air. They all felt the same. I kept going, and then I felt it. Electricity. My hand and the jewel started to glow. So this was the all-powerful jewel. It didn't look very remarkable at all. Looked like Umma's engagement ring, except this one was way bigger.

I breathed hard. The air seemed to be getting thinner. I gently placed the jewel in between the two dragons. The jewel began to shimmer, and it grew so bright, I had to shield my eyes. A whirring sound came from inside the dragon, and the jewel lifted itself up from the dragon's mouth and floated toward me.

I started to feel faint, but I held out my hands and caught it. It felt different. It was hotter than before and was somehow a lot heavier. When I looked closely, there was also something swirling around inside. I definitely hadn't seen that before.

I couldn't breathe. The hourglass. I stared at the hourglass on the shelf and saw a little bit of sand left. Then

I remembered that I'd forgotten to set it as soon as I got inside.

I grabbed the remaining half of the dragon's scale from my pocket and stuffed it into my mouth. Just like it had before, the scale melted in my mouth. My eyes started to droop, but I smiled weakly when I saw my foot turn to liquid.

I gasped for air and crumpled to the floor.

CHAPTER 22

The cold, hard ground jolted me awake. My eyes flew open, and I struggled to breathe. As I sucked in air, my lungs burned and I clutched my chest. I heaved and coughed but couldn't bring myself to get up.

When my eyes focused, I saw the chandeliers dangling from the ceiling of the ballroom.

I'd made it.

Wait. The jewel! I frantically patted my body. Where did it go? I remembered holding it as I passed out. Oh, please, please be here. When my fingers touched the pointy edges of the jewel lying on the ground next to me, I breathed a sigh of relief.

The Dragon King hovered over me, so close that I could almost see my reflection in his eyes. I groaned and sat up slowly. "Welcome back, Hwarang Lia." He stood up and adjusted his robe.

My body ached when I tried to stand up. "Never a doubt. Right?"

He smiled and reached out his hand. "Of course. You are the Hwarang, after all."

I let him help pull me up. My head spun, and I clung to his arm.

I coughed. It felt like something was still stuck in my throat.

"The scale will do that to you." He whacked my back three times, but it didn't help. It only hurt. I yelped in pain and scrambled away from him.

He held my arm and pounded my back again. "You need to get it all out or you'll turn into water forever."

I just stared at him. *Say what?* How come no one had warned me of this teeny, tiny side effect? Not that it would've stopped me, but it still would've been great to know in advance.

"What's supposed to come out?"

"You'll see. Hopefully." He used his fists now to hit my back.

All I felt was pain at first. After a couple minutes, though, my stomach fluttered. I covered my mouth and coughed and coughed. When I opened my hands, two carps with beautiful orangish-yellow scales swam out.

I couldn't believe what I was seeing. Never had I imagined I'd see a day where fish flew out of my mouth. I coughed again and three more came out.

"Five more to go. Make it a big one."

As if I knew how to do that. I cleared my throat, took a deep breath, and let out a bout of coughs. Tears formed in my eyes, and I couldn't catch my breath. But it was all worth it when the remaining five fish flew out of my mouth. I reached out my hands to touch one, but it flitted away.

"Am I good now?"

"You'll be fine," he said as he stretched out his arms.

I wiped my mouth and asked, "What are they?"

"Golden carps known for their color. Ten of those turn into one dragon scale."

I nodded as if I knew what he was talking about. One by one, the fish began spiraling around the Dragon King's arms.

The fish flew onto the Dragon King's robe and settled into the golden dragon emblem.

"Come, follow me." He turned around and started walking across the room.

I wanted to scream and shout. I'd just had things flying out of my mouth. And how cool was it that this powerful dragon actually had something so magical and beautiful as flying fish on its back? I trailed behind him. "Where are we going?"

"Back to your world, of course." He half smiled and said, "Did you want to stay here?"

"No thank you, Your Majesty."

He opened a wooden door with dragon-shaped brass handles. "After you."

I walked through and froze. This couldn't be right. Trees, grass, flowers, and pebbled paths . . . in the middle of the ocean? How could there be a park here? This was pretty much a giant greenhouse under the ocean. Somehow everything was protected by a huge dome that looked like a sky.

Looking at my confusion, he chuckled and said, "This way."

I bent down to touch the grass, and to my surprise, it felt prickly and soft like the real thing. This was some next-level magic. We walked down a pebbled path to a sandy beach. I slipped off my shoes and dug my feet into the sand. It felt warm and familiar. Just like the beach we used to go to back home. I trudged through the sand until my feet felt wet. Waves lapped gently onto the shore.

The Dragon King pointed to the ocean. "This is the entrance and exit."

I stared out at the water, but it didn't look familiar. "Are you sure? All I remember is a gold road."

He bent down and touched the sand with his hand, and it began to glimmer. "You mean like this?"

I gasped as the sand turned golden and shimmered just as I remembered.

"Is there a boat?"

He laughed. "You're a funny one."

I dipped my feet into the water and took a deep breath. Back to swimming for me.

"Put your shoes back on."

Who was I to argue? I jammed my wet feet into my shoes. The ickiness didn't even bother me today.

He knelt down and ran his fingers through the water. He whispered something to the water, and it glistened in reply.

"One question: How am I going to know how to get back?"

He stood up and pointed at the water. "Just relax. The waves will take you."

This made no sense at all. But nothing here did. I bowed farewell and walked into the water. The waves circled around my body and formed a cocoon around me. I didn't even need to hold my breath. Instead of panicking, a powerful sense of peace came over me. It was as if the waves were telling me that everything was going to be okay. I relaxed and let the water envelop my entire body. Before I knew it, I was in a capsule made completely of water. I touched the top and was surprised that it felt stiff. Not like water at all.

The waves pushed the capsule forward, deeper into the ocean.

I looked down at the jewel in my hand. So this was what Gaya was after. If I handed it over to her, there was no doubt in my mind I'd be sealing our fate. But even if I didn't give it to her, she'd still kill us all anyway.

Would it be so bad to use some of the jewel's powers just this once to save my family? It wasn't like I was the evil one bent on destroying the world. I was the protector, trying to save us all.

If the jewel truly helped the owner power up like the books said, maybe I had a chance.

A couple minutes later, the capsule opened and my body was being lifted up by a wave onto the same cliff I'd jumped off yesterday. It dropped me on the grass and disappeared back into the ocean.

I stood up to see Gaya walking toward me from across the field. "I see you found the jewel."

I hid it behind my back. "Where's my family and Joon?"

She snapped her fingers and showed me the holographic image of them. "There you go."

I laughed. "That's not good enough. No way I'm handing this over for that."

She crossed her arms. "You don't trust me?"

I snickered. "Not in the least. Bring them all here now."

"Give me the jewel first."

I moved away from her. "No."

She sighed and waved her hands. "I'm dealing with a juvenile."

My family and Joon appeared next to Gaya. They still had their mouths gagged, their feet bound, and glowing handcuffs on their hands. My heart ached seeing them in distress.

I peeked behind me and watched the jewel change colors, turning darker shades of gray until it was completely black. Just as the Dragon King said, as soon as Gaya appeared near me, the jewel activated itself for destruction.

But the longer I stood here, the clearer my decision became.

I reached into my pocket and gripped the red coin. It had once taken me to my halmoni's house. Maybe it could do that again.

Gaya caught on and said, "I told you, you're not strong enough to do that kind of magic."

"Oh yeah?" I wanted to prove her wrong.

She snarled, "Hand me the jewel."

"Sure. One second," I said.

I traced the symbol on the coin with one finger and gripped the jewel with my other hand, wishing with all my heart that my family, Joon, and I were all safe in Halmoni's living room. In a matter of seconds, the jewel grew warm in my hands.

This had to be a good sign.

Please work.

"Stop! If you do this, I'm going to burn everything down," Gaya yelled, and lunged at me.

A gust of air and a flash of light later, I stood in Halmoni's living room. My heart skipped a beat. That meant it had worked, and my family and Joon were here! I kissed the jewel and shoved it and the coin into my pocket. I whirled around and tears streamed down my face as soon as I saw Umma. Standing next to her were Appa, Halmoni, and Joon.

Umma ran to me with her arms still cuffed. I raced toward her and wrapped my arms around her. I snuggled my face into her shirt and breathed in the familiar Umma scent. She smelled of her favorite flowery peony perfume, just as I remembered.

I took everyone's gags off.

"Let me look at you." Umma smiled at me with glistening eyes.

I hugged her neck and said, "I'm so sorry for everything."

I'd been wanting to say that forever.

"It's okay. We're all together now."

"Looks like we're missing out on this reunion." Appa nudged me with his elbow.

I ran over to group-hug the others.

Joon wiggled out of the hug. "You're suffocating me."

Umma looked down at her cuffed hands and bound feet. "But first you need to get these off us."

"Do you have the key?"

Umma smiled weakly. "No, it's magic. You have to use magic to undo it."

I shook my head. "Why can't you do it?"

She sighed. "Because these cuffs prevent any of us from using our powers."

"Your mom's right. You need to get these off us." Halmoni lifted up her arms.

I took a deep breath. "Okay, I'm ready. What do I need to do?"

"Imagine them coming off and say 'puleojigeora,'" Umma said.

"But I don't know that spell." This was a new one.

"It's okay. Just try it."

I closed my eyes, pictured the cuffs and rope coming off, and chanted, "Puleojigeora." But nothing happened. "It's not working!"

Umma stood next to me and said, "You need to be very specific in your thoughts and speak with authority. You have to believe it's going to happen."

I sighed. "It feels like a dream that you're coaching me on magic right now." How ironic coming from the person who'd forbidden me from using any kind of magic all my life.

"I'll explain that later. Right now you need to focus."

In a firm voice, I said, "Puleojigeora," this time with even more conviction.

Sparks flew, and with a clang, all the cuffs dropped to the floor, and the ropes came undone.

"Thanks, Lia," Joon said as he rubbed his wrists.

Umma ran to hug me. "I knew you could do it." She stroked my face with her hands.

I took out the jewel from my pocket and showed it to my parents. "Here. I got it."

Umma and Appa both looked at each other and nodded in silent agreement.

"We should've told you everything from the beginning," said Umma. "Maybe we should've trained you instead. But you have to know we were doing the best we could to keep you safe." She wrapped her arm over my shoulders.

My heart sank. So this was all because of me. This just confirmed what I already suspected: that I was the one who messed everything up by doing magic at Dior's party. That's why the sky looked all funny. If I hadn't done that, Gaya would've never found us. Everything was my fault. And it still wasn't over yet.

I wiped a tear from my face and hugged Umma. "I'm sorry for breaking the spell," I whispered.

She pulled me off her and said, "What are you talking about?"

I looked up at my parents with my lips trembling. "I

shouldn't have snuck off. And I got scared, and I accidentally let out some powers. I'm the one who broke everything."

Umma chuckled and put my hands against her cheek. "Oh, honey. It wasn't your fault at all. Gaya was getting stronger, so it was only a matter of time before the spell broke. And your magic blocker was already very weak."

There were two major questions that had been bugging me for a while. "Did Gaya ever come after you and Halmoni? How did you protect yourself?"

Umma answered, "Gaya's been after us, too, but our powers manifested later, and we were trained enough to protect ourselves from her."

"Also, she wasn't as powerful back then," Appa added.

"It was just the perfect storm," Umma explained. "The combination of you being born with your powers already manifested and her becoming much, much stronger. She sensed you right away."

I stared at Umma and Appa. "Really?"

So this wasn't all my fault?

Appa hugged me and kissed the top of my head. "Yes, really. We knew better than to leave the protection spell to the whim of a twelve-year-old."

I smiled up at Appa. "What? I'm super reliable and trustworthy."

A huge weight lifted off my chest. It was just a coincidence that the spell had broken at the same time.

I breathed a huge sigh of relief.

"We're so proud of you for learning your powers. You were even able to transport all of us here. Did you use the coin?" Appa patted me on the back.

I looked down at my hands and said in a quiet voice, "Well, actually . . . about that . . ."

"No. You didn't." Umma hurried over and checked my hair. She gasped and showed Appa something. "Look. She did."

I grabbed my hair and stared at it. A whole strip of my black hair had turned completely white. When had that happened? I hadn't felt anything.

Umma must have guessed what I was thinking. "When you use the jewel, you gain a little power, but you lose a little bit of yourself."

I turned completely pale, and my hands shook. What had I lost? Was it something important?

"You won't get back what you lost. But you're still young. There's so much time to grow." She hugged me tight.

"So I won't become a monster?" I knew it sounded unreasonable, but it was a legit worry.

"As long as you stay on the right path, you'll be just fine." Umma rubbed my back in circles.

I shivered as I thought about the last thing Gaya said to me. "Do you guys think Gaya would really burn things down?"

A thundering boom shook the house, and we ran to the veranda to see what it was.

We stared in horror at the scene unfolding before us.

CHAPTER 23

Flames engulfed buildings and quickly spread like wildfire in the direction of Bukak Mountain. Just beyond it was the Blue House, where the president of Korea lived, and all of downtown Seoul.

Umma wrapped her arms around me and squeezed me tight. I knew Gaya had it in her, but it seemed no one knew exactly what she was capable of or how strong her powers were. If she could just snap her fingers and set buildings on fire, how were we going to fight her?

And win?

But we had to try. I had to face her and destroy the jewel once and for all.

Appa placed his arm around Joon's and my shoulders. "We need to go help."

"I know. I'm ready," I said.

"Me too," said Joon.

Appa shook his head. "Not you two. Your mom and I will go."

I stared back at him with defiant eyes. "I have to go too."

Umma gripped my hands and said, "It's more important to us that you're safe."

"How am I going to be safe if Gaya can track me because I used magic?"

Appa chimed in, "Umma can do another protection spell around this house. It'll be temporary but long enough for us to defeat Gaya."

I turned to face my parents. "I'm sorry, but I won't stay here by myself."

Tears welled up in Umma's eyes as she stroked my back. "You don't know how important you are. You have to survive."

"I will. I'm fighting with you." I took a step back from her and puffed out my chest. There was no way I was going to run and hide. Especially not when everything was at stake.

Halmoni stroked my hair and smiled at Umma. "She's just like you."

Umma sighed and sniffled. "My brave little Hwarang princess. You've never fought a battle like this. Stay close, okay?"

I nodded. That was true, I didn't have field experience, but I was the only one who could destroy the jewel. My whole life my parents had protected me by hiding me away, and look how that turned out. I was done running away. "So how do I destroy the jewel?" Halmoni or Umma must know because they'd been the protectors of the jewel before me.

Umma looked away from the window and said, "Once the jewel turns black, you chant the phrase 'Yeoiju buseojigeora.'"

Jewel. Break. That sounded simple enough.

Umma warned, "It's going to take a lot of focus, so don't be distracted."

I didn't know how I was going to do that in the middle of a battle, but I would need to figure out a way to empty my mind. "Okay. I will try my best."

Joon looked at me and said, "There is no try, only do, Lia."

I hated when he was right.

Umma closed her eyes and scooped at the air with her hands. Two jars appeared in her palms, one purple and one orange.

"What's that?" I reached over to grab the orange jar.

Umma quickly closed her hand around it and handed me the purple one instead.

"I don't have time to explain everything to you right now. But this is yours."

I opened the jar and stuck my finger inside. Rubbing my fingers together, I studied the texture of the purple substance. It was creamy, not as powdery as eye shadow but not as thick as paint. It looked a bit like body paint.

Halmoni handed Umma a white jar. "Hurry up and sit down. We don't have much time."

Umma opened the jar and took out a powder puff. She patted my face down, and I coughed as white powder flew into my open mouth. Then she took the purple jar from my hands. "Close your eyes."

"Can't you explain while you're doing this?" I couldn't understand why putting makeup on my face was so important. What could be more important than going out and fighting? Like, right now?

Halmoni explained while Umma continued to paint

my face. "It's so people will know who we are. Orange means Hwarang. Purple means the Hwarang leader of different clans."

My voice squeaked. "I'm the leader?"

"New generation takes over once they turn twelve. But under the supervision of a guardian until they turn eighteen."

No way. How was I going to lead anything?

Umma added quietly, "When Hwarangs paint their faces to go to battle, there's another reason, called nangjanggyeolui."

I didn't know what it meant, but the serious tone she was using was unnerving. "And that means?"

"It's a sign of resolve. That Hwarangs are willing to fight to the death."

That was a pretty loud statement, and I really, really hoped it wouldn't come to that.

The paint slid easily over my eyelids. Umma dabbed it around the corners of my eyes and around the bridge of my nose. I prayed I didn't look ridiculous. But maybe if she looked like this too, I wouldn't care as much. I opened my eyes.

"Keep them closed!" Umma barked as her fingers moved quickly over my face.

"The final touch," said Halmoni.

Umma tugged my chin down and ran something smooth over my lips. *Wait. What?* Was she actually letting me wear lipstick? I'd been dying to try it but got shut down every time I'd asked.

"Okay. You can open your eyes now," said Umma.

I opened my eyes and raced to the bathroom. *Daebak.* What stared back at me was, uh . . . shocking, to say the least. My face was pale white, which made the purple shadow around my eyes and nose stand out. I couldn't even tell it was me anymore. I smooched my lips together and smiled. The red looked great, though.

Walking back to the living room, I called out, "Umma, are you sure it's supposed to look like this?"

I stopped in my tracks. Halmoni and Umma stared back at me in the same white makeup except with orange shadow on their eyes and noses.

I stifled a giggle. We all looked so strange. "Do we really have to go out looking like this?"

Umma laughed and said, "I thought I looked funny too my first time." Her smile disappeared, and she said, "But it's tradition before a battle."

Appa gathered everyone together. "We need a plan."

"Lia and Joon, use your Taekkyeon skills. Everything you know," Halmoni said. We nodded.

Umma clapped her hands together. "Okay. We'll all stick together and go to the Blue House first. Our mission is to find Gaya so that Lia can get close enough to destroy the jewel." She looked everyone in the eye. "Understood?"

"Ne," Joon and I shouted together.

Umma grabbed Halmoni's hand and then mine. "Everyone, join hands."

I held Joon's hand and squeezed it. He squeezed back.

Umma held a coin between our hands, closed her eyes, and chanted, "Cheongwadaero idong."

My body levitated and landed with a thud on the pavement. The Blue House was completely engulfed in flames. Fire-engine sirens blared, and people ran screaming in all different directions. Deserted cars lined the streets, making it hard for any help to come through. Police officers waved orange wands, trying to direct people, but no one listened.

It was total chaos.

Umma shook my arm. "Come on, Lia. We need to find everyone else."

"Who else are we waiting for?" I pointed at Joon, Halmoni, and Appa. Everyone was here.

"The other Hwarangs."

What? There were more? And they were here? How

she was going to find anyone in this mess was beyond me. But we followed behind her anyway. Once we were far enough away from the Blue House, Umma raised her arms in the air with her palms facing up. A beam of orange light shot up into the sky, and she stared up into it as if waiting for something.

Orange and purple lights appeared all over the sky. I gasped and pointed wildly at them. "What is that?"

Appa leaned over and said, "Hwarang makeup has special powers so that in battles the warriors can locate each other."

There was a large number of orange lights near us at Gyeongbukgung, the old royal palace.

Umma pointed at the cluster of orange. "That's probably where Gaya is. Join hands." Umma grabbed my hand and chanted, "Gyeongbukgungeuro idong."

We appeared in the middle of the palace.

Inside the courtyard, Hwarang warriors in the same face makeup as us fought the shadows. I clung to Umma's arm. She leaned down and kissed my head. "This is it. Go look for Gaya! But don't fight her on your own. We'll come and help." And she pushed me away as a shadow came slithering toward us. "I love you," she yelled as she blasted the shadow with a fireball.

I ran as fast as I could toward a gate at the far corner of the courtyard. A shadow swooped in front of me. I froze in place. A hand grabbed me and pulled me through a gate that led into the second courtyard. When I turned around, I was relieved to see that it was Joon.

"You followed me!" I hugged him tightly. "Weren't you supposed to go off with my parents?"

He shrugged. "What can I say? I'm a rebel. Couldn't let you have all the fun."

"Well, let's go scout the area."

Joon didn't move. Instead he stared intently at me and said, "I was going to say something before, but I didn't want to offend your mom and grandma." He stifled a laugh. "But your face."

My ears turned red and I mumbled, "It's tradition, okay?"

"I know, I know. I've only heard about it. But seeing you in it . . ."

"Oh my gosh. Cut it out already." Now I was getting annoyed. This was not the time to be laughing about my makeup. We were in serious fighting mode.

"Okay, okay," he said, still chuckling. "Let's go find Gaya."

"Come on." I ran through the second courtyard, toward

Geunjeongmun, the gate leading to the Outer Court.

"Lia! You can't just run out in the open!"

I turned back to yell at him to hurry up when a shadow materialized in front of me and wrapped its arm around my leg. I kicked and punched it with my arms, but the shadow only gripped tighter. Joon picked up a sword from the ground and swung it across the shadow's arm. The hand loosened and my leg sprang free.

I scooted back and hid behind Joon.

"Where did you find that?"

"It was on the ground by the gate." He held the sword tightly in front of him. "Some of the Hwarangs were fighting with swords like this."

It must be a magic-infused sword. That totally made sense. Only magic could kill something magic. No amount of Taekkyeon would hurt these shadows.

We stood in front of Geunjeongjeon, the Throne Hall. Thank goodness I was right about its whereabouts. This was a building in the Outer Court, and it seemed like the perfect place for Gaya to be. Someone who wanted to act like a god and destroy our world. Everyone else must've thought so too, because as we got closer to the building, all we could see were Hwarangs fighting shadows.

"She's not here." I scanned the courtyard.

"This place is massive," Joon said. "How are we ever going to find her?"

I held Joon's hand and started to run. "I got an idea."

"Where are we going?"

I pointed to a little hill next to the building. "We might be able to spot her from up there."

We trudged up the hill and looked down at the palace. There were Hwarang men in makeup dead on the ground. Others were brandishing their swords and slaying the shadows. I tried to search for my parents and Halmoni, but I couldn't find them. I clenched my fists and walked to different areas on the hill to get a better look.

"I'm sure your parents and Halmoni are fine."

"What makes you so sure?" My voice squeaked but I didn't care. I couldn't lose them again.

Joon patted my back and said, "They're supposed to have been legendary agents, remember?"

I nodded. I wanted to believe him so bad.

He pointed to firefighters right outside the palace gates. "I'm more worried about that."

I followed his finger and stared in disbelief. The firefighters were using hoses to put out the fire, but they weren't working. The fire kept burning and wouldn't go out.

"It's got to be magic fire," I said. "That's why it's not working."

The entire city was burning. It jumped from building to building. But in the distance there was one structure with a different-colored fire. It was almost pink. "Look at that, Joon! What building is that?"

"That's Sungnyemun."

"Sungnyemun? The large gate in the center of the city?" I remembered passing by it on the bus ride to Seoul Station. "That must be the source." I smacked my forehead. "Why didn't I think of that?"

"Think of what?"

"There's only one gate with a vertical instead of horizontal name panel. Back in the day, horizontally placed panels were the standard."

"So?" Joon asked.

"During the Joseon dynasty, eight gates surrounded the city. Since Sungnyemun was one of the major entrances, the king ordered the vertical panel to be placed on that specific gate to protect the city from fire."

I bet he wished he'd paid more attention in IMA class. From here, it was impossible to tell if the panel hung correctly or not. "There's only one way to find out if it's really magical," I said.

Joon squinted his eyes and said, "I bet it is."

The cotton-candy-like pink flames engulfed everything except the two pointed tips of the roof. "That's probably why it's designated as national treasure number one."

He raised his eyebrows, clearly surprised that I knew about that. "You know what? You should just teach the next class."

A smile crept onto my face. Maybe a little bit of Appa's genes had rubbed off on me.

"Come on," I yelled as I ran down the hill toward the gate that led to the street.

He panted and said, "All right, genius. So how are we going to get there? It's not like we can take a cab or a bus."

The streets were a complete disaster. There were cars and buses abandoned all over the road. With people running in all directions, even if I could hot-wire a car, it'd be impossible to try to drive it without crashing. Plus I had no idea how to drive.

As I ran past a coffee shop, I spotted something in the alley. I stopped abruptly and ran toward it.

Joon followed after me, shouting, "You're going the wrong way."

Five electronic scooters stood parked against the wall of the coffee shop.

He leaned against the wall to catch his breath. "There's no key."

I took off my backpack and rummaged inside until I found my black pouch.

"Don't tell me you got something else in that magic bag of yours."

"You know it." I felt validated for carrying around an extra pound of stuff in my bag every day.

I finally found what I was looking for and pulled out a bobby pin.

"That's your solution?"

Whatever happened to silver linings, optimistic Joon? "Quit complaining and take out your phone."

He pulled out his phone and tried to hand it to me.

I waved his hand away and pointed at the key box on the scooter. "We just need to get inside that and connect the wires."

He just stared at me like I was speaking a different language. "How in the world do you know stuff like that?"

I shrugged. "I just do." While he was practicing magic, I tried to find other ways to make myself useful. Indispensable.

I stuck my bobby pin in a crack on the key box. "Use your phone and hit the pin, okay?"

He lifted the phone and was about to strike using the front.

"Stop!" I turned the phone in his hand. "Use the side of your phone unless you really want to break it."

"Right," he said, and then smashed down on the bobby pin.

The back panel of the key box popped open, revealing a panel of wires.

"Light, please," I said.

He turned on the flashlight on his phone and shined it on the box.

Inside, there were red, green, blue, black, and white wires. But only the red and green ones were disconnected. I tied the two together and checked the display screen. It blinked red and then switched on.

Joon clapped his hands. "Wow. That was impressive."

I flashed double peace signs at him.

While we worked on the next scooter, he said in a pretend serious voice, "I solemnly swear never to make fun of you again for being a wannabe MacGyver."

The second scooter whirred on. "That's right. You'd better not."

I stood on the scooter and examined it. There were only two options: a lever on the right and a bicycle brake on the left.

"You ready?" I shouted.

He zoomed ahead of me.

I pressed up on the lever and the scooter started to move. I swerved slightly to avoid crashing into a woman running across the street. The trickiest part of all this was navigating through the sea of people and randomly parked cars.

When we reached Sungnyemun, we stopped and parked our scooters near a tree.

I pointed at the pink fire. "Do you see that?"

"You mean that it's burning?"

"No." I turned his head to the left. "Look there. The sign. It's not there."

"Where did it go?"

I really hoped it was not in the fire, burning.

"It's probably in there somewhere."

He took a couple steps back and stared at the burning gate.

"I know how to fix this." He rolled down his sleeves and handed me the sword.

My heart sank. Why did he have to go and be a hero? I wanted him here, next to me. Alive and in one piece. "We can figure that out later. Let's go find Gaya first."

He nodded. "You're right. First things first."

Our mission. We needed to find Gaya so I could destroy this jewel. The faster I did that, the faster all this would be over. That was the best way to make sure Joon didn't run into the fire to try to save the day.

CHAPTER 24

People scurried away and deserted cars littered the streets. The shadows hadn't made it to this area yet. Maybe they were all congregated at the palace. Building after building caught on fire and people rushed out, some carrying the wounded.

But there was no sign of Gaya.

I raised the jewel above my head and shouted, "Gaya!" But the crumbling of buildings and people shrieking in terror muffled my voice.

The jewel began to turn gray. I swiveled around and scanned the area for Gaya. She must be nearby for it to change colors, but I couldn't find her.

With a swoosh, Gaya flew down from the sky and landed in front of me. "Give me the jewel, little girl."

The jewel grew black and heated up in my hands as Gaya drew closer. It had been activated now that she was near. I held it tighter in my hands. "Never."

"You Hwarangs," she sneered, "always want to do it the hard way."

She stretched out her arms and water spurted from the sidewalk, pushing my body into the air. My sword clattered onto the ground. I kicked my feet, but that only made my body rise higher. Then she closed her fists and something that felt like a wet, watery hand squeezed my neck. I coughed and heaved as it closed tighter. I tugged at the thing around my neck with my free hand, but that only made it worse.

I gasped for breath.

Joon picked up my sword and raced toward Gaya. He slowed down as he got closer to her and hobbled over in pain.

With the last bits of strength I could muster, I whispered, "No, Joon. Stop."

But it was too late. Gaya whirled around to face him.

The grip on my neck loosened and I toppled to the ground. I wheezed and tried to catch my breath.

I watched helplessly as Joon swung the sword at her.

Gaya clutched her chest with one hand and flexed her other hand, wrapping him in a tornado of water. Then she threw him into the burning Sungnyemun gate.

"No!" I screamed, and raced toward the fire.

Something wet gripped my legs and pulled me off my feet.

"You know it's all your fault that your friend is burning. If you'd just given me the jewel when I asked nicely . . ."

Tears streamed down my face and an anger I hadn't felt before burned inside me. "You monster!"

The sword lay on the ground in the spot where Joon had been right before Gaya had tossed him into the flames. I just wanted revenge. "Umjigyeora." I summoned it to move toward me.

Gaya smirked and stepped on it. "So you've learned a little magic, have you?" She jeered. "Too bad you're still no match for me." She stretched out her arms and muttered something different under her breath. It was an ancient form of Korean that I didn't understand.

Chills ran up my spine and water enveloped me, lifting me up. I dug my heels into the ground but it continued to drag me toward her. In desperation, I chanted the same spell to remove the grip as before, but this time nothing happened.

Gaya cackled and mocked me with her big black eyes. "You can't use that one anymore. I've blocked it."

What? There was such a thing as blocking? Why had no one mentioned this very important defensive skill?

I stood in front of Gaya, unable to move. She smiled and patted my cheek. I cringed at her touch and spit in her face. She wiped it off with the sleeve of her dress. "Really? Still such a child. You stood no chance against me, little girl."

Gaya swiped the jewel and, without even touching me, threw me across the street. My back thudded against a parked car and I yelped in pain.

She knelt down, raised the jewel in the air, and chanted in ancient Korean. Even though I didn't understand it, I knew what she was trying to do. I couldn't let her turn back time. The minute I stood up, I winced as pain shot up my leg. In the fall, I must've twisted my ankle. It was painful to put any weight on it.

The jewel rose into the air as Gaya's chants grew louder and more intense. The ground flickered and the cement began to fade away, revealing grass. Storefronts changed one by one to trees. People screamed and clung to each other as everything around us shifted. I stared down at my hands in horror. My fingers were disappearing, like ashes.

I needed to stop this. Or everything as we knew it would

be destroyed. Everyone would turn into ashes. Like they'd never existed. Time seemed to slow down as I watched my world change. But what could I do? I didn't even have the jewel anymore.

You are the true owner of the jewel. That was what the Dragon King had said.

I was the owner. And I should be able to control it. Because it was mine. As long as I could get close enough to her . . .

Hypnotized by the jewel's power, Gaya didn't budge from her position and continued to chant in a monotone. It was too painful to walk, so I crawled closer to her. I fell on my face. When I looked down, my right arm had vanished.

I couldn't stop myself from screaming.

Gaya turned around and the jewel dropped back into her hands.

I gathered all my strength and knelt before her. "Please. It's not too late. Please stop this."

"I've waited too long." She closed her eyes and held the jewel up in the air again.

I cringed as I blurted out, "The king and your baby wouldn't have wanted this."

That definitely got her attention.

She swiveled around and glared at me. "What wouldn't you do for your family?"

Tears streamed down my face. I'd do anything for my parents, but this was different. "I'm sorry for what my ancestor did to you. But you going through with this is only going to kill more people."

She whipped out her arm and struck me in the head with a force so strong I couldn't move. "Silence, Hwarang! You know nothing about pain."

I whimpered and watched in horror as she began chanting again.

This was my only and last chance to destroy the jewel.

I closed my eyes and repeated in my head what Umma had taught me, "Yeoiju buseojigeora." I was the owner and I commanded the jewel to self-destruct. I imagined the jewel exploding and shattering into a million pieces.

Gaya shrieked as the jewel dropped into her hands and a white light exploded into the sky.

Feeling powerful, I continued to chant louder and with more purpose. "Yeoiju buseojigeora."

She flung out her arm toward me again. This time I shouted to protect myself, "Boho!" A power field appeared around me and deflected the lightning bolt she shot at me. Furious, Gaya gathered her hands together and aimed a ball of fire at me. I squeezed my eyes shut and hoped the protection spell would hold. I breathed a sigh of relief when the fire sizzled and extinguished as soon as it neared me. My spell was working.

I bit my lip and continued to chant, "Yeoiju buseojigeora."

Without warning the jewel exploded and tiny little pieces flew into the air. The force of the blast was so strong, it broke through the force field and threw both of us onto our backs. I cringed and covered my ears, which had started ringing like crazy.

Destroying the jewel drained all the energy out of me. All I could do was lie down and stare up at the stars as I strained to take a deep breath. A couple feet from me, Gaya groaned in pain and struggled to get up. This bought me a little time to gather strength before getting up to fight Gaya again.

I checked the front and the back of my hands and wiggled my fingers. All ten fingers accounted for. A slow smile spread across my face, and I relaxed my body.

It had worked.

I had destroyed the jewel. The ground had returned back to regular old cement. I never thought I'd be so happy to be lying on the sidewalk.

The abandoned cars on the streets flickered and

reappeared. And the buildings stood just as before.

This wasn't over, though. I needed the sword to destroy her. "Umjigyeora." I held out my hand and the sword flew into it.

I used the sword as a crutch to get up.

Gaya was on the ground, but she held on to a small bottle that glowed a neon blue. It was the one that used to be tied around her waist.

That must be the source of her water powers.

I charged at her with my sword in the air.

Watery arms came at me, but I slashed at them with my sword. As I drew closer, Gaya inched back and the bottle slipped to the ground.

I smashed the bottle with my sword and watched the blue liquid spill out. It then disappeared down the street and into the sewers.

Gaya was so weakened she could hardly get up.

This was my moment. I raised the sword and yelled, "And this is for Joon!" I wanted to make things right for him. But I couldn't bring myself to kill her. She was a pathetic mess and so weak. Joon wouldn't want me to stoop as low as her.

"You're not worth it," I said as I lowered my sword. I turned to walk away.

But wait.

Why wasn't the fire going away?

Now that the jewel was destroyed and Gaya's powers had weakened, shouldn't the fires stop too? Yet as far as my eyes could see, the fires raged stronger than before.

All of a sudden, Gaya shrieked as a brown half-circular pendant floated toward her from Sungnyemun Gate, which was still burning. She reached out to grab it, but it glided out of her reach. I squinted my eyes and moved closer to get a better look. I couldn't make out all the details of the pendant, but it looked just like the half-circle birthmark Joon had.

Gaya winced as she pulled herself up and hobbled toward it with outstretched arms.

The second it was in her hands, she started to weep. She placed the pendant against her chest, and the other half floated out from inside her. The two pendants swirled around each other in the air, leaving a trail of pink dust. They seemed to be tracing an invisible symbol gliding up, down, and across. The dust settled, revealing the hanja for the word *love*, and then the two pendants snapped together.

I stared in disbelief. How could the pendant that looked just like Joon's birthmark match perfectly with whatever it was that came out of Gaya? Was it really Joon's? And if it came out of him, what did that all mean? Was he alive? Dead?

Gaya clutched the unified pendant and wiped her face with the cuff of her sleeve. She yelled, "Agaya, Umma yeogi isseo," as she hobbled into the fire.

My baby. Mommy's here.

I gasped and covered my mouth with my hand. Joon was the baby she was looking for? But how? It didn't make any sense. Joon already had Ajumma and Ajeossi. Not to mention Gaya was probably centuries old, absolutely ancient. But Joon was just like me.

My age. And from my time.

I wished with all my heart that by some miracle he'd be okay. He just had to be.

It felt like an eternity, but Gaya finally emerged from the fire, cradling Joon in her arms. I didn't know where she found the strength to carry him when she could barely stand up a few minutes ago.

She laid him gently on the ground before collapsing next to him. He had a metal bar poking out of his chest. I screamed and tried to run to him, but Gaya pushed me away. She had enough power left in her to pin me to the ground.

Joon's face was smeared in soot, and red welts covered every inch of his exposed skin. He lay there gripping the broken pieces of the panel in his hands. Gaya leaned over and wiped his face with her fingers.

Tears streamed down her face and dropped onto his. She kissed his forehead and whispered, "Uri yeppeun aga, Ummaga neomu mianhae."

My beautiful baby. Mommy's so sorry.

Straining to sit up, she stretched out her arms over his body. Her arms tensed and shook before she dropped them to her sides. Crying, she pressed her face next to his and wailed, "Uri aga eotteoke. Eoseo ileonageora."

It was so hard to hear her words. *Wake up, little one.*

Please, please get up, Joon.

Gaya yanked out the metal bar, and blood gushed from his chest.

My heart felt like it was being shredded. I knew this must be the fatal wound Joon couldn't heal himself from or he would be joking around, showing off the panel and how he saved the day.

She pulled out two binyeo, hair sticks, from her braided updo and placed them on the ground. They looked like thin little daggers with butterflies sitting on a circular green jade stone where the hilt should be. She picked one up and ran it across her palm. Blood trickled down her arm, but Gaya didn't flinch. Instead, she placed her hand on the wound on Joon's chest.

I didn't know much about magic, but that looked like blood magic. It only worked between blood-related family members and must be performed by someone very skilled in the dark arts. And it required a sacrifice. Not quite a life for a life, but you had to give up some of your powers. It could kill you if you were already really weak and didn't have much left to give.

Gaya hunched over him and her back heaved up and down. I couldn't take my eyes off Joon's body as it rose into the air and rotated around like chicken on a spit. His arms and legs jerked and then stiffened. A lightning bolt appeared out of nowhere and struck his chest. Joon's eyes snapped open, and whatever force that had been holding him up laid him back down.

Joon gasped and took in a deep breath.

Gaya lifted her head and stroked his face. "How are you here? I've been trying to find my way back to you forever."

He cringed and tried to inch away from her. "Get away from me!"

Gaya sobbed and knelt down beside him. "I'm so sorry I couldn't recognize you. Could you ever forgive me? For hurting you? For trying to kill you?" She pulled out the pendant from her pocket and showed it to him.

Joon stared at it and lifted his shirt up. "How did my birthmark get there?" His arm flailed as he reached out to grab it.

"It's me. Umma." Gaya steadied his arms and placed the now connected pendants inside his hands. "This was sealed with love. I gave you one half of it when you were born and placed it right here." She patted the area by his collarbone. "So that I could find you again."

He took the pendant and tried to pull it apart.

"But I have parents."

She stroked his hair. "I know. They raised you well. So strong and brave."

Gaya couldn't stop crying as she leaned down to hug him. "I've been searching for you over all my lifetimes. I'm so sorry, baby. I never expected to find you here." She drew back to study his face and traced his eyebrow with her finger. "How could I not have recognized you? My own son."

"You should've known." He groaned and rubbed his collarbone where his birthmark used to be. "It was on fire whenever I was near you."

Tears dripped down her face. "I felt it too, but I was blinded by hatred. I didn't realize what it meant."

Joon turned his head away from her and grunted as he tried to get up.

She pressed his shoulders down. "You need to rest some more, my little one."

He groaned again, but he listened to her. "How can I be the one you're looking for if you were born centuries ago? It's not possible."

Tears dropped down Gaya's face, but she held her head up high. "I did what I had to. To find you. I'd do it all over again."

"What did you do?"

She turned her head away from him and said, "I found a way to take souls. The first time was hard. But it worked and made me live longer."

Joon reached his hand up to touch her face. "But what did you sacrifice? Black magic comes at a cost."

Gaya wiped her tears and smiled. "Little slivers of my soul. But it was all worth it. To see you now."

"You have to stop. I'm right here."

Gaya nodded. "I can't believe you've been here all along."

"Wait. If I'm ancient like you, how am I even here?"

She smiled and pointed at the pendant still in his hand. "Because of this. When I placed it in you, it gave one of us—you—the power to regenerate."

"Uh. You mean like a lizard? Haven't tried chopping off any parts of my body, but I don't think so."

She chuckled. "No. Not like a lizard. I mean you have many lives. You probably grew old just like everyone else, and then you were reborn with your memory wiped clean."

He sat up and rubbed his temples. "That's crazy. I can't believe my parents never told me about that."

"They probably didn't know. It's a very special and rare power."

He took a few shallow breaths and rubbed his collarbone. "Since I don't have the birthmark anymore, does that mean I'm . . . ?"

She nodded. "Just like everyone else. This is now your one and last life to live."

Joon placed the pendant on the ground and coughed. "I can't breathe."

She helped him lie down and cradled his head in her lap. "You need to rest."

A loud, thundering boom shook the ground. We swiveled our heads to the sound and watched in horror as a building toppled over. Thank goodness it was pretty far away or we'd have been completely squashed. All around us, the flames grew stronger and the buildings began to sway. Fire seeped out from the cracks on the buildings and slid onto the sidewalks, setting them ablaze.

Gaya shielded Joon with her body. She stretched out her arms and yelled, "Fire, I command you to stop."

But the fire grew even stronger.

She stood up and raised her arms even higher. "Meomchugeora!" But whatever she was doing drained her energy, and she crumpled to the ground.

"I don't have my medicine bottle anymore," Gaya said.

Joon held her hands and stared up at her.

Gaya panted and said in between breaths, "My power's too weak."

The sidewalks were now a sea of fire. People clambered on top of cars to keep safe. A couple sat in a tree and reached down pull a little girl up.

Joon and Gaya huddled together as the fire crept toward them. She drew him close to her chest and wrapped her arms around his head.

Tears rolled down his face as he said, "Thank you for using your powers to save me." Then he showed her the panels he had brought out from the fire. "Maybe these will help."

"Is that what I think it is?" She picked up a broken shard and studied it. "I thought I smashed it."

"You did. That's why it took me so long to find all the pieces."

Gaya rearranged the pieces so that they resembled the original panel again. She ran her fingers over it.

But nothing happened.

"I can't anymore. I'm so sorry, my love."

When he didn't answer, she looked down at him and patted his face. "Wake up, wake up!"

Joon blinked his eyes and smiled weakly, "Don't worry about me. I can heal myself now."

She collapsed next to him and whispered, "I'm so sorry."

Joon wrapped his arms around her and cried. He looked over at me and said, "And let her go."

Gaya snapped her fingers, and immediately I was able to move my body again. I ran over to Joon and hugged him. "You don't know how happy I am to see you."

He smiled weakly. "Me too."

I didn't know what to say about Gaya being his biological mom. All I could do was hug him and weep with him.

After a while he pushed me away. "The fire."

I wiped the tears from my face. "Right, the fire."

I held the two broken pieces of the panel in my hands and pictured them together. "Butigeora." I was just resparking or regluing the things that used to be together.

I held my breath and watched in anticipation as the pieces wiggled closer to each other.

Just a little more.

Little sparks of fire started falling from the sky. I dodged one that landed near my head. They were small enough that they went out as soon as they landed. But with enough of them landing, it was only a matter of time before the whole city would go up in flames.

I closed my eyes to block out everything and focused on the panel. I chanted, "Butigeora."

Stick together.

The edges of the broken pieces began to glow. I concentrated and spoke again in a firm, commanding voice. One by one they snapped together like magnets.

"I always knew you could do it," Joon said.

Gaya turned to face me and nodded. I didn't know what to make of that. Maybe that was her acknowledging what I'd just done. At least we were past trying to kill each other, for now. There were much bigger things to worry about, like the end of the world.

She let go of Joon and picked up the panel. Before getting up, she looked straight at me. When I looked into her now brown eyes, they were different. The coldness and hatred were gone. In their place was sadness. She pointed at Joon, and in a voice choked with emotion she said, "Take care of him."

I fought back tears, but I knew what she meant. I had used up all my energy putting the panel together, I could barely stand, and Joon hadn't fully healed himself yet. She was the only one among us who could move. It had to be her or we'd all be doomed. We all knew that to stop the fire the panel needed to be put back. No one had enough energy to use magic. Someone would have to physically go and hang the panel back in its spot.

Joon clung on to the bottom of her dress. "Just wait. I'll be better soon."

She shook her head and said softly, "We don't have much time."

"But I just found out about you."

She kissed his cheek. "Let me do this for you."

He wiped the tears and winced in pain as he tried to sit up. "No. Please. I can be ready soon."

Gaya knelt down, picked up the pendant from the ground, and gave it to him. "Keep this close. I'll always find my way back to you."

Joon tried to stand up but collapsed back onto the ground. He called after her, "Umma. Saranghaeyo."

"I love you too, my son. Always and forever." She turned

around and smiled at him one last time before disappearing into the burning gate.

I hobbled over to Joon. We sat in silence, staring at the gate.

I squeezed his shoulders and hugged him tightly to let him know I was here for him. A simple *I'm sorry* didn't seem enough for all the emotions he must have been feeling right now. What can you say to someone who just lost the mother they'd never known they had? My heart broke thinking about how Gaya went into the fire to make things right so that her son could live.

The fire started to disappear and smoke billowed up into the air.

In a choked voice, Joon said, "She did it."

"I know." All I could do was hold his hand. I didn't have any words to make him feel better about this.

Even though we knew there was almost no chance of her coming back alive, we still waited and hoped. But there was no sign of her.

"Umma! Umma!" He tried to stand up, but I held on and hugged him. Joon eventually stopped trying to fight me and sobbed into my shoulder.

I rubbed his back the same way Umma did when I cried. "She really loved you."

Joon wiped the tears rolling down his face. "I just wish

I had some more time with her." He groaned and looked at the gate, which was completely burned down except for the panel propped vertically against what was left of a wall. "At least she did the right thing."

"Yeah, she did," I said softly.

I hummed a song Umma used to sing to me when I was little to calm me down. Joon leaned his head on my shoulder, and we sat like that for a while.

In the distance we heard people calling our names.

"Lia! Joon!" Appa came running toward us. Close behind him were Umma and a swallow flying over her.

"Is everyone okay?" Umma asked.

I couldn't help but blurt it out. "Did you know Joon's real mom was Gaya?"

They stood frozen. "What? How can that be? Are you sure?"

Joon cleared his throat and said, "It's a long story. We'll debrief you on the way home."

Umma furrowed her eyebrows. "We didn't know about Gaya. But Joon is special."

I nodded. "We know. Gaya told us."

"Only the senior people at the agency know. That's why Joon's family lived in our neighborhood, where we had the protective spell," Appa chimed in. "To keep him safe and out of the spotlight until he was old enough."

We filled them in on Gaya's sacrifice.

Umma stared down at my hands. "And where's the jewel?"

"I destroyed the jewel," I added.

Appa embraced us both. "I'm so proud of both of you."

Halmoni winked at me and said, "Don't you think they're ready to attend IMA school next year?"

Umma smiled and squeezed my shoulders. "They've definitely proved their worth."

People dressed in white robes appeared everywhere. They stomped their feet and chanted.

I stood next to Umma as I watched. "Who are those people?"

"They are memory-alterers. Normal people can't handle everything we know. So this is how we protect them."

The people in robes continued to stomp, and then the ground began to rumble.

"When they are done, everyone will believe there was a giant earthquake in Seoul."

All the normal people around us rubbed their heads and looked around as if in a daze.

Appa put his arm over my shoulders. "Ready to go home?"

CHAPTER 25

The weekend was a whirlwind of sleeping and de-stressing by eating and watching a marathon of Korean dramas with my parents at a giant suite at a hotel back in California. Temporary housing provided by IMA, of course. Even though we couldn't go back home, it still felt the same because we were all together. Best of all, only a couple more weeks were left of school, and then summer break. My parents promised we could go back to Korea and visit Halmoni, though she warned me that it would be sweltering hot.

I squinted and looked over at the alarm clock. It was already seven a.m. Waking up in the morning, especially on a Monday morning, used to be tough, but today was different. Umma had agreed to teach me basic spellmaker skills before school every day. I thought she wanted to make sure I knew enough to protect myself. Which was kind of ironic, considering how against it she was before. With good reason, now that I thought about it. I got ready for school in record time and bounded out into the living room, where my parents were waiting for me.

"So what are you going to teach me today?"

My parents chuckled. "Good morning, Lia."

"Morning." I sat down between them.

On the coffee table was a package addressed to me.

"What is this?" It didn't look like the usual packages that came to our house.

They looked at each other and smiled.

Okay. Something was going on. I picked up the box cutter and sliced the edges.

As soon as I opened the box, blue balloons floated into the air. There were probably at least twenty of them. How had they all fit in the tiny box?

Umma pointed inside. "There's more!"

I stuck my hand inside and pulled out a blue camping flashlight, the ones that could stand up on their own. A little arrow pointed to the button on the side.

I pushed it. On the wall I saw the hanja for *east* and a blue dragon.

No way.

"Does this mean I got in?"

My parents got up to hug me.

"You did! But there's one more thing in the box," Umma said.

I reached inside and pulled out a thick plastic card with a string attached to it. It looked like an identification tag that I'd wear around my neck, except there was nothing written on it.

I rubbed it with my hands, and words in black ink started to appear.

It read *International Magic School, Student: Lia Park, House of Benevolence.*

"Oh my gosh!" I squealed, and jumped up and down. This was the best news ever.

"Congratulations, Lia! We're so proud of you," said Appa.

I looked down at my card and beamed. "What about Joon?"

Appa grinned. "Why don't you ask him yourself?"

The doorbell rang, and I ran out to open it.

Joon stood there smiling ear to ear with an identification card around his neck too.

We gave each other a high five.

"So which house are you?" I hoped we were in the same one.

He showed me his identification card. "House of Courage."

I wasn't sure how they picked who went to which house, but courage seemed fitting for him. Even if we weren't in the same house next year, I was happy that I'd found a true friend, and somewhere I belonged.

ACKNOWLEDGMENTS

Being a young Korean American girl in the eighties and nineties meant that the heroes in mainstream fiction books did not look like me. I didn't realize until I was much older that my endless appetite for reading was in part a search for a leading character who shared my story. Lia Park is the hero I hungered for, and it took so many people to help make her a reality.

First, thank you, God, for your love and grace through every step of my life. You are my greatest source of strength and hope. I count each blessing in life from you with deep gratitude.

Thank you to my agent, Penny Moore. In my mind, you wear a cape and fly around like a real superhero. Thank you for tirelessly advocating for representation and diversity while being my business guru, staunchest cheerleader, and warm friend. I'll never forget that first call with you, and I'll always be grateful to you for believing in me and the story of Lia Park.

Thank you to my brilliant editor, Alyson Heller. Your sharp eye and editorial insight helped bring to life a character that I hope will inspire many young girls, and many young Asian American girls, to take pride in their

ACKNOWLEDGMENTS

background and know that differences create strength. Thank you for celebrating the spirit of Lia's story and teasing out the details that magnify that spirit.

Given my master's degree in Korean art history, the cover art was important to me. I wasn't sure how an illustrator would be able to capture the intricate details of the Silla dynasty while also fully expressing Lia Park's spirit. Hyuna Lee, you did all of that and more. Thank you.

Thank you to Heather Palisi for taking all the stunning visuals and words and creating a jacket that somehow looks better than the individual parts.

A huge thank-you to Valerie Garfield, Kristin Gilson, Chelsea Morgan, Ginny Kemmerer, Sara Berko, Alissa Nigro, Jenny Lu, and the entire team at Aladdin and Simon & Schuster for all your dedication, passion, and commitment to bringing this book to life.

This book was written while I was pregnant with my second daughter and caring for my first, a toddler at the time. To beta readers Appa, Alicia Yoon, Edward Scott, Erica Ishigaki, Jomike Tejido, Kristina Schwartz, and Rebecca Matthews Vorkapich, your input was invaluable, and your enthusiasm for the story was fuel for me during many, many late nights. Thank you, thank you, thank you.

ACKNOWLEDGMENTS

Last but not least, my heartfelt thanks to all my family and friends for your friendship, love, encouragement, and shared laughs and tears. You have sustained me over the years and especially during the pandemic as I was completing this book.

Thank you to my Zoomies, Miri and Sanli. Your friendship and prayers are tremendous blessings. You've been with me through so much of this publishing journey, and your support and encouragement have meant so much to me.

To Eddie, my amazing brother-in-law and fellow coffee aficionado, thank you for reading my earliest draft and being so supportive of my writing. I'm grateful that I could always count on you for a good laugh and kindness. Thank you.

In particular, I'd like to thank my grandfather, who passed away this year. Even though he never got to see the final version of this book, I know he would be so proud. When I was growing up, he often told me, "You are Korean. Help your Korean community." I'm honored to have the opportunity to write books with Korean main characters so Korean kids and the Korean community can be seen and celebrated.

To my umma and appa. Thank you for believing in

every single one of my dreams no matter my age and no matter how big or small the dream. And thank you for teaching me that I could achieve anything, even if it wasn't always the most conventional path. Gomawoyo, saranghaeyo.

To my sister, Alicia, thank you for being my best buddy all these years. We used to dress up and pretend we were the superheroes in our favorite books. Thank you for reading every single draft and for encouraging me to develop a superhero who doesn't require quite as much pretending. I'm so blessed that you are my sister.

To my husband, Bud, thank you for being my best friend, my sounding board, my brainstorming partner, and my most fervent supporter. Your unwavering belief in me, Lia Park, and this story made all the difference. Thank you, love.

Finally, to my beautiful daughters, Mihee and Taehee, I hope you grow up knowing that everything is within your reach. Anything is possible, so dream big and discover all the magic within you. You two are my inspiration and the reason I write. I hope to create a better and more inclusive world for you. I love you, my wondrous girls.